# REFLECTIONS OF FEAR

Robert Cosper

# CONTENTS

# 1

## CHAPTER 1

With death at my doorstep, I had to muster up the courage to do what seemed impossible. With all my strength, I took a breath, ignored the searing pain in my temple, and—

"Eyes wide open."

My eyes nearly rolled when those words dropped from his lips. Just the thought of Nolan gazing at me and knowing my mind had been elsewhere irked me. He knew me too well, judging by how I stared off into the distance at nothing. Still, my lips pouted and softened while I reestablished my focus on the soft white lights ahead and the click, click, click of the camera.

Only me and the athletic yoga pants hugging my lower body were in the shot against the sickly white backdrop that showcased my natural light brown skin my online fans adored. Time to sell my soul by selling the controversial leggings that had been dubbed the "colorist pants" by so many online in the fashion community.

By becoming the new representative for SSL, I was showing all the cool kids that a multiracial woman could sport Salty Saddles Leggings too. I knew rocking their clothes in an ad would only prove the company embraced people like me because of our racial ambiguity. I was aware that consumers wished to see the likes of a dark-skinned beauty sporting the leggings and not just a light-skinned woman of color with an ethnic background like me. I couldn't help but wonder if consumers would see through SSL's halfass attempt to calm the backlash of the current scandal.

"Extend your elbow and arch your back," Nolan ordered, his British accent breaking through his acquired American one. Of course, I complied. After all, he knew how to contort my body in ways that not only pleased each of us in bed but the masses in a photo. I trusted him to keep me feeling and looking good. It was our job, our livelihood depended on it.

From the corner of my eye, I could make out the attractive dimples on his smooth cheeks and my heart fluttered out of habit even as I told my brain to focus on the task at hand. At the start of our relationship his authority was a turn-on. He would order me around the bedroom with a no-nonsense attitude we both enjoyed. It had been a sexy tactic we used to keep the bedroom unpredictable and fun.

But outside of the bedroom—?

"More cleavage." His fingers snapped, stealing the attention from the monotonous clicking of the shutter. "Eyes on camera."

I hadn't looked away from the lens since he reminded me to extenuate them by opening them more, but I hugged my chest tighter to further push my breasts up into perfect mounds, determined to keep the perfect shot obviously meant for the male gaze. But wasn't our goal to sell pants to the teenage girls that mostly made up my fanbase?

Why question it? If it worked, it worked. And I had learned a while ago not to question a business's intentions. They knew exactly what they were getting when they hired me. It wasn't far-fetched that they had a team of talented experts who studied what their target audience wanted and the best way to sell it to them. The money wasn't coming in because I pointed out their morally ambiguous or inept decisions. After all, they were paying me to sit still and look pretty. So, sit still and look pretty became my expertise.

"That's it, baby. Beautiful."

A sense of pride swept through me from successfully suppressing an eye-roll. The pose was excruciating, but he, the photographer, or the viewer would never know. Not showing my pain was a skill I developed years ago, and it made me determined to make sure the viewer, the consumer, and even the most critical fashion enthusiast wouldn't see my pain either.

My career, my boyfriend, my life—I knew I had plucked a four-leaf clover and I had no intention of letting it wilt.

After a few more shots, Nolan called it done. I couldn't be more thankful for the break as it seemed like work was a nonstop endeavor. Even sitting in a makeup chair for an hour had begun to be exhausting.

I sighed, craving three things: privacy, a nap, and a double bacon cheeseburger. At least one of the three were possible.

"What's going on in that pretty little head of yours?" Nolan winked as he placed an off-white terry cloth robe around my shoulders, allowing me to embrace some sense of privacy and warmth in the chilly room. His large blue eyes filled with concern. "You seem a bit off today."

"Nope." I flashed a smile, feeling my cheeks tightened as I exaggerated the grin. "Everything's peachy."

"Peachy cobbler?" He raised an eyebrow, questioning how sure I was.

"Peachy cobbler." I nodded, hiding a bashful grin that threatened to sneak out every time his thick eyelashes fluttered. No matter how much he angered or annoyed me, all he had to do was give me a wink and a smile and it prevented the issue from sinking in too deep.

With a hand on my lower back, he guided me across the large, open space to sit at the small desk in the corner of the room. I would have had a serious issue being in a windowless room if it wasn't so spacious and bright with large theater lights to simulate natural lighting. Many companies rented and used the space not only for private photo shoots but for art and fashion exhibits as well, making our photography setup seem minuscule in comparison. Even so, the large lights anchored on the beams in the ceiling only emphasized the immenseness of the area.

I sat before the laptop that I used so many times to connect to my fan base around the world. We made sure to bring it with us to the studio and everywhere else we went as it was an important part of the job. I was well aware that keeping a healthy connection to my fans was vital to the advancement and relevance of my career. Without them, I might as well not exist.

"I want to show you how beautiful you are." He snapped his fingers before gliding them across my cheekbone to push a strand of hair behind my ear. This time, Joselyn's high heels click-clacked on the linoleum floor as the first sign of her presence. The steady click, clack emerged from behind the white backdrop and the set of umbrella lights, and she approached with the camera in hand.

Out of habit, I tapped my finger on my knee. A rhythmic beat on the pads of my fingers. Nonstop. Unconsciously at times. Was it a nervous tick? A sign of impatience? A prelude to the annoyance threatening to burst out of me? I wasn't sure. Maybe all the above. Either way, I couldn't afford to lose it. I had to keep it together.

Joselyn walked up, and I flashed a smile, always aware of my resting bitch face. She returned the grin. "Nolan? Rhea?" I hated the dress she had on. It wasn't the fabric or style that put me off but how her hips filled it out perfectly. No matter how much Nolan insisted he loved my petite frame, I'd often catch him eyeing Joselyn's shapeliness whenever she walked away. His eyes rarely lingered on me when I stroll away. I've checked.

So, which is it, Nolan? You like thin or curvy? I wished those words came out, but instead I tucked them away with the other whiny, complaining parts of me that would make me look like a jealous type. No one liked an envious woman.

"Show Rhea how well she did." Nolan gestured to the camera. His well-manicured hands and slender fingers stole my attention. A visible yet subconscious sign of health and wealth. His attractive hands. No matter how many times he hurt my heart with his wandering eyes, his touch never failed to make up for it. After all, he could look but those hands only ever touched me.

"Oh yay! Pics." She crouched down, angling the camera for me to see the screen. The ends of her blond ponytail came forward to frame her face. And suddenly she took on the childlike demeanor that would match her age if she were ten years younger.

But before I could focus on the raw images, a wispy darkness in the corner of the room took my attention. When I looked beyond the white lights and their umbrellas that softened them, a hazy, blackness stretched into the shape of a torso with limbs, and my breath caught when an ethereal humanoid figure looked back.

Startled, I yelped and stood, accidentally knocking the camera from Joselyn's hands and to the floor. The clink-clank of heavy plastic colliding with the white tile floor stunned me, but not enough to force me to pull my sights from the figure in the corner. "Sorry, sorry, sorry." I placed my hand over my chest to steady the rapid beating of my heart, but to no avail.

"Rhea!" Nolan hissed.

"I'm sorry." I kept my eyes on the corner where the dark shadow faded, further blurring the edges of its translucent lines into nothingness.

Was my mind playing tricks on me? What did I just witness?

I blinked to clear my eyes of any impurities that could have disrupted my vision. Still, I couldn't make sense of it. What the hell was that? The tiny hairs on the back of my neck tickled as they stood on end, and suddenly the air around me grew colder than it was before.

Even now, as I focused on the corner and the weird, misshaped fogginess that slowly dissipated, I could make out the humanoid form. How much of what I saw was real and how much was my eyes playing tricks on me?

"What's wrong?" Nolan patted my lower back to soothe my nerves, but his touch only startled me more. "Rhea?"

Do I say it? Do I allow it to just fall from my lips unfiltered? Would being honest in a time like this make me strong or vulnerable, and should I care?

I shook my head, staring in the distant corner. "Something's the re..."

**2**

CHAPTER 2

Nolan and Joselyn turned and followed my line of sight, staring at the same spot on the opposite side of the room. When I glanced at Nolan, he shook his head in annoyance. "You're trying to deflect, aren't you? You're willing to create an issue because you want to call off the live stream today? Listen, babe. I understand you've been working super hard these last few weeks, but this upcoming week is the most important of your career."

"It's not that, Nolan." I secured the robe, clutching it tighter at my chest. I knew I should not have opened my mouth about it, and of course the vulnerability rushed in. "I thought I saw something. It scared me, but it's nothing. It's fine."

He sighed. The steel blue in his eyes complimented his short, slick, dark hairstyle perfectly. "I didn't mean to get snippy, babe." He pulled me forward by the nape of my neck to kiss my forehead. "We've all been work horses lately. You forgive me?"

"Yes, I forgive you." I glanced at Joselyn who stood by silently, waiting patiently with her lips tightly pressed together. Was that an attempt to keep from putting her foot in her mouth and saying something she couldn't take back later? Was that confirmation that she sided with Nolan and his theory? "A shirt would be nice, Jos."

"I'm on it!" She clicked her tongue as she turned to leave the space. "That's what an assistant's for, after all," she mumbled as she disappeared around the corner and into the hall.

I couldn't give her any shit. Not only did she make a great assistant, for the few months of getting to know her, I always looked at her as a friend. A sister. A confidant. Although we were nearly the same age, the power dynamic between us–me hiring her and technically being her boss–always made me feel like the older sister.

I lay my head on Nolan's shoulder, feeling his defined muscles through his button-down shirt on my cheek as I took in a whiff of his subtle name brand cologne as if it were aromatherapy oil. I knew where his eyes roamed and what they had locked onto but decided not to let envy be another thing rattling around in my head. If only his scent contained properties that enhanced mental and emotional health and wellbeing. "I think I need a rest."

"I agree." He kissed my forehead again. The pale, smooth skin of his chin grazed my nose and I allowed my eyelids to close to let his comforting touch sink in. "But we have the live stream in less than an hour. I want you pumped, excited, lively. They want to see you at your best. Always."

Of course, "pumped, excited, and lively" was a part of the business of UpTube. You had to not only be entertaining but engaging at all times, never let your audience get bored. Never let their attention slip. And sell, sell, sell.

"Yea, yea." I huffed. A dull pain throbbed my right temple. "But maybe just a quick twenty-minute power nap?" My palms registered the hard muscle of his pecs as I persuaded him with my touch. "It'll help. Trust me." I gave him the look that usually prompted a 'yes' out of him while putting a growing knot in his pants.

"You're killing me, babe." He leered. "Off you go."

I grinned and he sent me off to nap with a firm smack on the ass.

My only intent was the bed in the fully functional suite across the hall. Why else would he book this studio and the adjacent suite if we weren't meant to use the bed and the amenities over the two-day weekend?

I convinced myself Fate wanted nothing more than for me to nap at this very second. I was sure whatever I saw in the corner of the room was the sign I needed more lengthy and substantial relaxation.

On my way across the massive room, built to accommodate a huge production of several sets and multiple models and their crew in one space, my shirt dangled on Joselyn's arm as she handed it to me before I exited. "Thanks, Jos," I called over my shoulder.

The ache in my temple increased as I entered the cozy suite and strolled past the Multiracial Award placed on the counter of the kitchen bar. I sighed, shaking my head at the diamond shaped decoration as I remembered being honored with that ridiculous oversized hunk of glass.

A groan escaped me every time I read "Rhea" etched alongside "top multiracial fashion influencer" on the glass. All I had to do to win such an honor was surpass the sixty-million follower count on UpTube and contain at least two racial backgrounds within my genealogy.

It wasn't the years of hard work on the online platform, the many people that looked up to me as a role model, or even my savviness as a twenty-four-year-old entrepreneur in the fashion industry that gave me the nomination and eventual win. It only took possessing Native American, African, European, and East Asian genes.

Tragic.

The king-sized bed called to me, and I answered by flopping on the pillow top mattress, full face on and all. The headaches, stress and residual anxiety were locked away by the red satin sheets. The ease of slipping under had never been more real.

Finally, at what should have been peace, an eerie darkness crept in. Sleep should have felt good, warm, and welcoming, instead a sense of dread swept over me.

The blackness surrounded me in a nightmarish cloak, nothing like my usual dreams of peer praise, career success, and personal achievement. Uncomfortable was an understatement, especially since I was lucid even while slipping under. Darkness and a steady breeze of chilly fog enveloped me. Where was I and why in my lucidity did I end up in such a dreadful dreamscape?

In my search for something to bring meaning to the dark empty environment, my vision adjusted to the nothingness until an obscure figure caught my eye.

The thin feminine shape contrasted against the blackness behind her. Long, rusted-colored, wavy hair floated around her still attached to her head like the snake-like tentacles of Medusa. The strands hovered about as if she were suspended under an ocean of water. She stood as tall as me. Her five-eight frame reminded me of Mom, familiar, especially the broad shoulders and slender hips. I haven't spoken to Mom in a few weeks, was this my guilty conscience punishing me for my inaction?

The more I stared, the more uneasy I became. Was she facing away or looking at me? It was hard to tell judging the silhouette. But one thing I knew for sure, she was coming closer, moving so slow it could be mistaken as floating. Her head tilted as if questioning, as if cautious and skeptic, as if I were the intruder of her dreams.

My eyes never left her although the logical part of me urged me to wake up even as she glided closer, closer, closer. Curiously, I fought that urge and waited, anticipating what would happen next.

Curiosity took over and I stared, pushing away the fear that pushed back.

My mind raced. Why did my dream feel so real? Why was I seeing this figure? What does it want or symbolize? According to my extensive research in high school, and the subject of my study, the famous psychologist Carl Jung, my psyche must have been trying to communicate some very important things I couldn't grasp.

Just as I let my guard down, the dark figure rushed forward bringing an icy cold wind that nearly stopped my heart. "Run!"

My eyes opened and immediately stung as a bead of sweat dripped from my forehead and into the corner of my lid. I wiped the moisture with the back of my hand, feeling as if time hadn't passed at all. Had I been out cold for a few minutes? How could my body produce so much sweat in such a short amount of time?

I flipped over in bed to hear Nolan's British accent in the distance as he spoke with energy and excitement, talking about how eager he was for me to showcase the latest fashions in the upcoming event. While I anticipated Joselyn's response to his words, that eerie dream kept replaying in my head.

I reminded myself that all dreams are a form of release. Everything that happens in a dream is symbolism for everyday experiences, according to the tons of Carl Jung books I've read on the subject over the years. So, what was this weird dream symbolizing? Was it merely a representation of my guilty conscience for severing ties with my parents, Mom especially? Or was it hinting at my secret urge to "run" away from it all and become integrated into society as a regular person?

Something I wasn't ready to admit publicly, and not even to myself at times. Why would a person in my position ever want to give up a career like mine. I was the proud owner of a figurative four-leaf clover.

My attention went back to the conversation Nolan was having in the studio and how Joselyn never responded to him. In fact, she hadn't said anything since I opened my eyes. I let my eyelids close to better focus on Nolan's faint words.

"I'm telling you all, Rhea can't wait to see you guys. We're both extremely excited to be a part of this. She can't wait to kick off Up-Tube's Fashion Week. So let her know you wish her well by tapping that like button..."

"Oh, my god. The live." My heart skipped at the thought of sleeping through the highly anticipated livestream.

I sat up and a scream tore from my lips when my sights landed on the same wispy figure from my dream. This time she stood motionless at the end of the bed, looking directly at me with wide eyes. My breath caught in my throat when I recognized the features of the face looking back at me. They were my very own.

# 3

CHAPTER 3

The scream that ripped from my lungs burned my throat as it exited my mouth. Clutching the sheets in my fists helped anchor me as my first instinct was to squeeze my eyes closed at the unbelievable sight. I peeked through the slits of my eyelids to witness the dark apparition blend into the shadow of the decorative tree snug in the corner.

Before I could let the silkiness of the sheet's satin fabric register in my palms, Nolan was at my side, rocking the bed as he crawled onto the mattress. "Babe? What's wrong?" His comforting palm caressed my lower back, easing my shock and simultaneously urging me to speak.

The more I stared at it, the tree's shadow looked more like a real shadow and less like an odd, black mist a strange ghostly figure left behind. Still, it did nothing to calm my nerves.

"Something was there, looking at me." I didn't tear my eyes from where she had appeared. "A woman. I could've sworn it was a woman."

"Oh, babe." He sighed and as his breath escaped his lips, I read the skepticism all over it. "The nap didn't help, yeah? I figured it would have since it was so difficult to wake you. You know you missed the livestream?"

My eyes watered with hot tears that refused to drop. "You don't believe me."

His slender fingers caressed my chin, urging me to turn and gaze into his deep blues before he planted a soft kiss on my aching temple. "You're overworked. I get it. I'll let you get away with it this time, but we must keep our promises for the fans." He backed away, causing me to rock as he left the bed. "In fact, as your manager, it's my job to hold you to your schedule and your obligations. Unless there's a real emergency—"

"I'm telling you I saw a woman standing there." I wiped my eyes with the back of my hand, feeling the searing tears sting the rims of my lids. "She looked just like me."

"Aw, babe. You sure it wasn't a dream?" The sound of him tinkering with objects near the kitchen captured my senses. "You have the tendency to get riled up before big events."

I thought about the last gala I attended and how mentally unprepared I had been to simply walk the red carpet, and realized Nolan had a point. I had just awakened from a dream of the shadowy doppelganger. It wasn't too far-fetched for me to wake up believing I had seen her in real life. I rubbed my eyes with my knuckles, being mindful of the false eyelashes barely gripping the corner of my lid. "You're right. I'm such a mess right now."

"Maybe you're coming down with some sort of bug," he suggested, absentmindedly staring at the diamond trophy on the bar counter. "Complaining of headaches, sleeping in the middle of the day— I almost thought I would never be able to wake you."

"Yeah?" I stretched, feeling my rapid heartbeat slowly drop back to normal. "How long was I out?"

"I don't think the sponsors would be too happy, but you missed the entire thirty-minute live stream," he confirmed.

What? How could that be? "But I went down nearly an hour before the live stream."

"Exactly. I tried to wake you. I mean, I shook you, pulled your arm, I even tapped your pretty little cheeks several times, but you refused to budge." He went to the fridge, probably to fetch the wine he had stashed for celebration. "We'll have Joselyn schedule you an appointment with your doc, but after the weekend." He emphasized "after" with his British accent.

"Can't we just have Dr. Desirée make a house call?" I massaged my increasingly throbbing temple. "She can come out to me. She's on our payroll for a reason."

The commotion from the kitchen stopped, and I turned to see what had caused the silence. Nolan tilted his head and stared at me unblinking. Not even a strand of hair out of place. "There's so much to do over the next two days, Babe. More promo shoots. Another live stream tomorrow with the whole Q and A. I mean, this weekend is entirely booked."

"Yeah." I nodded, getting out of bed. "You're right. It can wait till Monday." I don't know what was going through my mind. Of course, Saturday and Sunday would be super busy, and I couldn't spare twenty-minutes for a doctor to look over me.

Of course.

I stashed away my irritation and tried to do the same with the anxiety and fear that remained since the nightmare. It didn't make sense to linger on my pain, the dream, or what I saw at the foot of my bed. And I sure didn't have any intention of causing Nolan and Jos any undue stress during our time here.

"Listen." He placed a couple of empty wine glasses on the counter. "I'll have Joselyn set you up with the doctor first thing Monday morning." He cleared his throat. "Hey Jos?" he called out to her, and his British accent grew stronger with the height in volume.

The click-clack of high heels announced her presence as she pushed the door open and entered the room. Bright white light from the studio across the hall lit up the space behind her. "Hey, guys! You rang?"

I sighed, reluctant to make a big deal out of my issue. "Can you schedule an early morning meeting with Dr. Desirée for Monday? My head is killing me." The throbbing was relentless and no matter how much I tried to not let the pain grasp my attention, that became the one thing I focused on.

"Aw, the stress getting to you?" She frowned, her shoulders dropping to portray her disappointment. "You're gonna do great like you always do. So many people's heads are gonna explode when they see you on that catwalk next week. You got this, girlie."

"Yeah, I know." I huffed, trying to ease the subtle ache that traveled from my head to my neck. "I'm just physically beat."

She frowned. "I get it. I'll get you set up with Dr. Desirée early Monday. Is there anything else you need before I head out?"

"That's everything." Nolan nodded.

"Alrighty." She waved, twiddling her manicured fingers in the air before pulling the studio keycard from her name brand purse. "See ya tomorrow." She turned and closed the door behind her. We listened to her receding footsteps as she crossed the large studio and exited the building.

As soon as she left, I went to my neatly stacked bags and suitcases in the corner of the room near the sofa and coffee table. I searched my purse for my cell phone but only sunglasses, a pack of mints, lip gloss and other junk stared back at me.

"Can I help you find something?" Nolan offered.

"Yea, I can't find my phone."

"I have it here." He pulled it from his pants pocket in a seductive motion that reminded me why I enjoyed his hands so much. With his sensual swagger, he made his way around the bar counter before placing it in my palm. "What's the issue?"

"No issues," I said while taking the phone. "It's just, the woman. I saw her in my dream, and she reminded me of my mom."

He paused, stuffing his hands deep into his pockets, changing his demeanor from spicy to arctic in seconds. "You're not calling her, are you?"

"Well, I thought I'd just check in..."

"No offense, Babe, but that woman is psycho," he scoffed, shaking his head in disapproval. "This is nothing new to you."

"Yeah, trust me. I agree, I just thought—"

"I mean, she doesn't support you or your career, your decisions, and especially our relationship. Much like my own folks." His jaw clenched, further highlighting his chiseled jawline.

It wasn't unusual that we were both dealing with parents who refused to be a part of our lives, each for different reasons, but mostly due to the direction we decided to take regarding our careers and love life.

"You're right," I sighed, rubbing my temple, trying my best to rid myself of the flush of embarrassment and frustration, "and I really don't want to remind you of what you went through with your parents—"

"Then don't." He shrugged and went back to the kitchen.

I stared at the phone in my hand, debating if I should continue the conversation and try to explain or change the subject.

The only contact I've had with Mom was around six weeks ago when I had been invited to walk the catwalk for UpTube's Fashion Week alongside other fashion influencers. All the excitement due to the event being streamed live she turned it into dread when she made it clear she had no interest in watching or supporting.

"Not as long as you continue to let those people treat you like a worn tampon," she had said. "They have only one use for women like you, and even though you perform to their liking, they'll eventually throw you out with the rest of the used trash." No matter how much I disagreed, she wouldn't budge. "That Nolan too. He's no different."

But she was wrong. Nolan had always been business oriented and serious about his work, and one thing he would never do was get rid of me. Right? He had been the one to encourage me to follow my dreams, opportunities be damned. He was the only one who told me, "If opportunities don't present themselves to you, create your own. Don't wait for others to tell you 'You have what it takes.' Show them." And ever since, luck has been in my corner.

I placed the phone on the coffee table and sat back on the couch. "I don't know what I was thinking."

Nolan smiled, showing off his cute dimples. "I know what you were thinking. You, my pretty, were thinking of doing an impromptu live stream to talk about fashion week and those sexy leggings you're wearing. Maybe we can save face with the SSL sponsorship."

I nodded, thankful for the potential distraction. Any distraction from the eerie figure of my dreams was a welcomed one. "Yeah, good idea."

# 4

CHAPTER 4

I tidied my makeup and hair using the camera on my phone, rolling my eyes at the live image it captured and reflected. I much preferred my professional makeup artist and his skills. My comfort zone involved coordinating outfits, picking suitable accessories, and otherwise sticking to the fashions. In other words, it meant staying in my lane.

Ready, I logged into UpTube, surprising my followers with a live stream. As the number of fans quickly rose into the tens of thousands, I smiled, putting on my welcome-to-my-wonderful-life face. My almond-shaped brown eyes and the expertly placed eyelashes grabbed my attention much like they've done the masses.

Beyond the forced smile and the intact veneer, I was aware of something bubbling beneath the surface. I couldn't put my finger on it, but a part of me didn't want to dig deeper in fear of discovering a harsh truth I wasn't ready to face.

Luck was on my side, especially since meeting Nolan fresh out of graduate school with a degree in business management. Luck was him seeing potential in me, taking a chance on what I offered, and putting all his skills into catapulting my career. Luck was falling in love with such a stunning, intelligent, boss-type who looked out for my best interests despite the ten-year age gap. What right did I have to complain when so many people would die to be in my position?

The comb of my hair extension dug into my scalp and I ignored it and widened my grin. "Hey, guys. It's Rhea here." My bright teeth lightened up the screen even if it was by slim contrast. "I just wanna pop in to say sorry for missing the live stream earlier. Let me tell you, fashion week is such a super big week for me and I'm doing everything to prepare and bring you all such amazing looks. I was so fortunate to have Nolan here to fill in for me earlier." I angled the phone to allow Nolan to lean into the frame. "Don't know what I'd do without him."

"Hey, guys!" His grin made me smile wider.

I watched the hundreds of messages scroll by in the chat. Most of the comments were different variations of the same thing.

"You're beautiful."

"She's so pretty."

"I heart Rhea and Nolan."

"Rhea and Nolan forever."

"Stunning."

"#Couple Goals."

Only a few messages dared to ask, "How are you feeling? Are you okay?"

"Aw, thanks, guys. Uh, I'm actually feeling..." I shook my head, absentmindedly rubbing my temple until I noticed and stopped. Portions of my dream replayed in my head—thick blood-red hair floating around the woman's head like tentacles—and I questioned how honest or cryptic I should be. I leaned forward, getting comfortable on the sofa. "Have any of you ever experienced something so unbelievable it made you second guess yourself?" Instead of searching the comments for answers, I continued. "I mean, you believe you have a good head on your shoulders. You're a smart person, right? You know you're making the right decisions, but it's like a guilty conscious or something that's keeping you from seeing what's right in front of your eyes? Well, maybe you see it, and you know it's there, but you doubt it, and feel like it's best to ignore it and move on?"

Curious to see if they could relate, I scanned the incoming comments as they zoomed by.

"Are you ok, Rhea?"

"Is she talking about her relationship?"

"We stan Rhelan! Rhelan forever!"

I imagined the viewers behind the keyboard and wondered what their young and receptive minds might have conjured up. Maybe they didn't understand, or worse, maybe they didn't care. They showed up for a good time, that meant they wanted fun and fashion. No one wanted to discuss serious matters at a time like this.

I didn't clarify their questions and concerns, feeling comfort in the fact no one besides Nolan knew I may have stroked out and began seeing things. There was no need to go any deeper than I had, anyway. I mostly needed to vent, to get those thoughts and feelings off my chest.

My eyes shifted from the comments, and I thought aloud. "I mean, I guess ignoring it would only do so much, especially if I know the truth. I must sound crazy, but..." I stared ahead at a misty, shadowy shape as it materialized in front of me. The faint outline of a humanoid body hovered feet above the ground. I shook my head and looked back at my phone, trying to stay focused on the task at hand.

The comments continued rolling in. "What's wrong, Rhea? Are you okay?" Over and over, messages filled with concern and curiosity scrolled by. "What's wrong with her? I don't think she's well. You look like you saw a ghost."

I shook my head, on the brink of letting it all spill out of my mouth, but knowing better. "There's just so much I wish I could share with you—" the phone disappeared from my hand before I could finish my thought.

"Nolan!" I stared at the phone in his hand as he turned it off without so much as a pause. "Seriously?"

"What are you doing?" He shook his head, frustration etched into his forehead with a couple of worry lines. "You're supposed to rectify your previous mistake. Not make new ones. Rambling on like that is going to make you lose your sponsorships. All the big brands."

"I was just talking, Nolan." I glared at the black screen of my phone in his grip. "When did talking become such a bad thing?"

"No, you were not just talking. You were going on a tangent about nonsense, and we can't have that." He huffed, pacing back and forth by the coffee table. "You need to remember you are a professional, not a fucking high school vlogger."

"What are you talking about? Why are you so angry?"

Talking to my fans and being personable, and even relatable, had always been a part of my brand. That's how I started on UpTube, by sharing my thoughts along with my fashions. There were probably many members of my audience that preferred I didn't share my thoughts, but regardless, that part of me had been a part of my time as Rhea since the start.

"You were gonna tell them about that woman you thought you saw." He paused and shook his head. "That's crazy, Rhea. We can't have your fans or the fucking industry elite thinking you're losing your mind. You know how important this week is to your career. You can't go around telling everyone you're having a mental breakdown."

A mental breakdown?

"I wasn't gonna say anything." I scoffed, not surprised that we couldn't go one weekend without an argument. The look on his face said so much. Did his intense stare come from a fear that I was getting sick or concern about the business? I extended my arm, displaying my palm. "Can I have my phone back?"

"I think I'll hold on to it for the time being." He pocketed it.

"You got to be joking." I waited for another angry remark, but he silently strolled back toward the kitchen instead. Maybe I would try a different tactic, using the magic word. "Can I please have my phone back?" I didn't know what I would do with it once I got it, but having my property back in my grasp had become my mission.

"I'm only looking out for you, Rhea." His calm voice took me off guard, although it was direct. "You'll thank me later."

My mind immediately took me back to an argument we had a few weeks ago. After I had made a batch of red chili chicken wings and invited him to sit down and enjoy them with me. Instead of indulging, he grabbed my plate as soon as I lifted a chicken wing from it and tossed the entire dish into the trash. His only explanation? "I'm looking out for you. Trust me, you'll thank me later."

"Nolan, give me my phone." This time, I put fire behind my words. "Just give it to me."

He paused, staring unblinkingly. "You want your phone back?"

"Yes."

"You want it back that bad?"

"Yes. I do."

He pulled it from his pocket. "Then bloody have it." He drew his arm back and pitched the phone through the air like a baseball. It met its target, landing in the center of my gut.

I buckled over from the sudden blow, clutched my stomach, and gasped for air. Not caring for the phone anymore, struggling for a proper breath had become my sole concern.

"Aw, fuck." He rushed to my side. "Sorry, Babe. I didn't mean to—"

I shrugged his hand from my shoulder and pushed him away as I made my way to the bathroom, where I closed the door behind me, locking it. He had promised, sworn, and vowed not to hurt me again. He lied.

# 5

## CHAPTER 5

With my back against the door, the four walls of the bathroom seemed to close in around me, swamping me. My hand kneaded the tender muscles where the cell phone met my gut and the pain slowly subsided. I listened to the regret in his voice through the two-inch wooden door that separated us.

"Babe, are you okay?" His voice was low but close enough that I could have sworn his lips caressed the wood. "I'm so sorry. I didn't mean to—my temper. I know, it's no excuse."

"Leave me alone," I groaned, bowing my head in heartbreak and shame, trying to gain the courage to go to the sink and look at the person I had now become.

"Rhea, baby," he pleaded. "I'm sorry. I love you so much. I hate that I hurt you."

"Go away." I shook my head at the unrecognizable face in the mirror; eyes smudged with mascara and eyeliner, eyelashes drooped on one lid, the symmetry of my beauty wiped away with just one blow. I peeled off the set of false lashes and dropped them in the sink. They lay on the slope like a pair of moths that flew too close to the flame.

When had I turned into such a foolish woman? Why did I choose to believe Nolan's words even though his actions spoke louder? Maybe what held me in place was the convenience of our partnership, the control he seemed to possess, the fear of change, or the ease and comfort of the familiar. Whatever it was ... "I can't do this anymore."

"Rhea, don't say that." He sighed and the door creaked. I imagined him leaning against the doorjamb, a shoulder anchoring his bodyweight. "I need you. You know I need you. You need me too. We need each other. I can't think of living life without you. I'd go crazy. I'd die. Please, open the door and let me talk to you. I want to see you—"

I turned on the facet and allowed him to ramble in the background of the swoosh of running water, and the steady stream escaping down the drain. The water reminded me of what it could do for all my negative emotions and the things I deemed exhausting, unworthy, a waste—wash them all away.

I glared at my reflection in the mirror. In a whisper, I told myself, "You're stronger than this. You're smarter than this. You deserve better than this. What are you doing? Why do you keep believing his lies?" I had to look away. I couldn't stand to see the worried, unsure, and unconvinced girl looking back at me.

And yet I understood.

Nolan and I found each other when we were up and coming in our respective professions, helping each other boost our careers. We gave each other purpose when our families chose not to support our business decisions. My parents despised social media, but I assumed it had been because it baffled them being an untraditional career. His parents thought he could do better as a lawyer or doctor and didn't approve of him managing a then nineteen-year-old on-line influencer.

And because of that, we understood each other, especially in our times of need. It became habitual and alongside the mind-blowing sex, we've become experts at listening, motivating, bonding, and eventually capturing each other's hearts.

I'd often joke that four years ago Fate had led me to the café where I had offered the dashing well-dressed man a coffee and added my UpTube handle on the coffee cup in black marker. The conversation it started led us to our present successes.

I remembered his sexy grin and deep cheek dimples when he said, "You know, back in the day we'd exchange phone numbers when we wanted to pursue a relationship."

"Is that your way of asking for my number?" I licked my lips before placing the straw of my iced coffee between them for a sip. The way he spoke, using big elaborate words, pulled me in. Alongside the ton of books I consumed, his way of speaking may have influenced my own vocabulary over time.

"Hmm." He sat forward, not a winkle on his clothes or skin despite him being at least ten years older. "I like your courage. Not afraid to go after what you want. I appreciate your go get 'em attitude. That's my kind of people."

I winked. "I would love to be your kind of people."

I turned the faucet lever until the water stopped and watched the pair of lashes disappear down the drain.

"Rhea? I'm such an asshole. I'm sorry." His voice made its way through the wood that separated us, soothing as his touch had once been, but dripping with sorrow that struck me as sincere. He meant every word out of his mouth. "You mean too much to me. Don't I show you that? Haven't I proved that to you? I can't believe I let my frustrations get the best of me. Just like you, I'm stressed too, and struggle to keep it together for you. For us. For your career. That's my job, right? Protect?"

I shook my head at my reflection. Confused at what I wanted and what I should do. On one hand, I wanted what we used to have. The laughter, the passion, the understanding. But on the other hand, I wanted it to be over. I didn't want to walk on eggshells or think about what I say and how I said it.

I wanted freedom.

Yet I knew, I felt it in my bones that my body would push every fiber of my being open that door and walk out of the claustrophobia of the bathroom if my mind wanted to or not. That habit had been formed over four years, and now I fought the urge to unlock the door and walk into open arms and sweet kisses.

Gripping the rim of the sink and focusing on the empty drain, I struggled to stay put. Finally, I peered at myself in the mirror, taking in the puffy red eyes that lured in so many, the glistening wetness that collected beneath my nostrils, and the utter mess I had become.

I quickly opened the faucet to scoop up a handful of the cold water before closing it again. And although my face craved the cool refreshing splash, I tossed the liquid onto the mirror and watched as it distorted my reflection. Another one of my strange rituals, much like the finger taps, and avoidance of tight, dark spaces.

Now I couldn't make out those almond shaped light brown eyes or the moisture that streamed from those eyes and down my cheeks no matter how hard I tried. I didn't want to see her. I didn't want to investigate her pitiful face and see her shame as she contemplated giving Nolan another chance.

But before the water completely cleared from the glass, large, scared eyes looked back at me, and the deep red hair of my reflection rose to float around the misshapen head. In seconds I realized it wasn't my reflection I was looking at but the ghost with my face.

I took a step back, staring at the distorted stream of bright red liquid as it ran down the side of her face. I froze in fear, anticipating her next move.

Her open palms repeatedly hit the glass, but her fluidlike movements prevented the sound of impact as well as her screams, but the visual of the ghostly figure and her gaped mouth overpowered my senses.

I screamed, quickly running out of the bathroom and straight into Nolan's arms.

"What's wrong, babe?" He glanced in the bathroom when I looked over my shoulder at the normal looking mirror. "What happened, love?"

"I saw her." My voice trembled as well as my lips. "I saw that woman again."

"Hey, now," his voice sent a calm through me and so did his caresses on my back and shoulders. "You're alright now. It's okay. I've got you."

I buried my face in his chest, pulling him even closer by the fabric of his shirt. "Something's happening and I don't like it." I held back a sob. "I want to leave."

"Of course. Of course." He held me snug, and an immediate sense of safety surrounded me. "Let me take care of you, yeah?"

I nodded against his chest, thankful that he was near but knowing I would regret it later. Did holding on to anger make sense at a time like this? I'd make sure to teach him a lesson later, but for now staying on his good side seemed like the better option, especially if he agreed on getting out of this place.

My mind flooded with warnings about what a stupid thing I've done running back into his arms but was quickly shelved by the eerie memory of the haunted face in the mirror.

My heartbeat caused the tips of my fingers to tremble as I moved strands of hair from my face. "I thought I wanted this. I thought I wanted to be here and prepare for fashion week, but after seeing that woman, all I want to do is leave. I just want to get out of here."

"Sshh." He caressed my shoulders. "Come now. Let me fetch you a drink." He led me to the bar where I sat at the counter while he rummaged through the fridge. My eyes continued to cut to the open bathroom door almost expecting her to come floating out the mirror like Bloody Mary.

The clink of wine bottle to glass caught my attention and I turned my sights to the noise. "Nolan, not now."

He continued pouring. "Let me apologize properly." The red liquid swirled in the cup, nearly mesmerizing me, or distracting me from the fear of what was to come. But then he paused, stopped mid-pour, and looked up from the wineglass. "You know, Rhea... I'd die if you ever leave me. That's how much I love you. And you don't want to see me dead, do you?" He shook his head. "Of course, you don't." With the bottle in one hand, he used the other to slide the beverage to me, a half empty chalice. "Now drink up."

**6**

**CHAPTER 6**

The satin bedsheet cooled my heated skin as I sprawled naked on my back. I appreciated the cool sheets as it contrasted the heat generated by the red wine flowing through my body. The bed rocked as Nolan climbed over me, the warmth of his skin against mine secured me in the familiar.

I allowed him to nestle between my legs while his body weighed me to the mattress. I had only a few sips of wine, but already the liquor shot through my veins and its heat throbbed between my legs.

Nolan's manly scent became delicious enough for me to crave his lips in a kiss. I expected his cool tongue to taste like aged red grapes, but it hadn't ... only sweeter.

In my mind, the words, "What are you doing, Rhea?" interrupted my pleasure. I pushed it away and focused on the power of his hips as he sank deeper into me. I let out a moan and he responded with one as well. With a few more thrusts his moans matched mine in rhythm.

Drowning in bliss, the sinister thought of our broken future was kept at bay even though it tried seeping in. I opened my eyes to pleasure-filled deep blues and slid my palms over soft skin and hard muscle. My aim was to drink him in through all my senses and let ecstasy rest there the way the sweet and dry flavor of wine rests on one's tongue.

I hoped to soak in the feeling and wished his pleasure would last forever, and replace all my fears about the future of our relationship, my mental state, and my career.

But as my eyes closed, she appeared. Her stringy red locks reached out like silky tentacles ready to wrap me up and drag me to hell.

I gasped and forced my eyes open, just as Nolan's head disappeared lower down my torso, leaving a trail of wet kisses and soft nibbles along the path. My lids grew heavy and I fought against the weight.

I focused on the magic of Nolan's wet muscle as I cradled his head between my legs. My own voice rattled in my brain, "You don't want this."

I argued telepathically with the voice, "He's happy. Making him happy keeps the pain away." I gave up on the struggle with my eyelids as the heaviness won the battle, and before I knew it, I was swimming in an ocean of darkness.

At first, the gentle rocking threatened to lull me to sleep, but like a baby on a treetop the bough broke and down I fell. The hollowness in my gut reminded me of the cellphone and its impact, but in no time, I realized it was the harsh sensation of free-falling that tugged at my insides.

Nausea overcame me, and suddenly trying to hold in my stomach contents became priority. Still, surrounded by utter darkness the feeling of dropping vanished and became replaced with a sense of floating.

I hated the darkness, but its vastness hadn't yet triggered the panic of claustrophobia.

Was I upright or upside down?

Was I here or there?

What was happening?

I looked over my shoulder at nothing at all, but far in the distance she stood. She too floated in midair, and for a split second I wondered if her body mimicked mine, like a mirror. Without a proper light source, I could only make of her face that it looked a lot like mine but different.

Her eyes were wide. Her mouth agape. Her head ... strange.

"You're broken." Her lips didn't move when she spoke, but her voice was clear. "You don't want this. You have to leave."

I shook my head in confusion. "What?"

"Now!" Her unearthly growl rattled my ears.

I sat up in bed, pushed Nolan aside, and tried desperately to catch my breath. "What happened?" Confused, I reached out for something to grasp and found Nolan's forearm. The dim lights from the kitchen lit up the space and slowly brought me back to reality.

Was I dreaming?

"You're fine," he assured me. "Take a deep breath. Relax. It's only the wine." His chest and shoulders glistened with sweat, and he struggled to catch his breath as well.

"I'm scared," I confessed, rubbing my temple that began to ache.

"You're fine." He stroked my shoulder. "I'm here, Rhea. I'll make sure nothing happens to you. Okay?"

I glanced around the room. I recognized the items, yet everything seemed unfamiliar. None of my beloved books sat on the bookshelves like they did in my room at home. The sheets and mattress didn't feel right and were less comfortable than my own. Even the smells...

I wanted to go home.

For some reason, I wanted Mom. I wanted to hear her tell me I was fine and everything would be okay.

"I don't know if I can do this, Nolan." I pushed myself to the edge of the bed to place my feet on the floor.

"Sex?" He shifted in bed. "Okay. We don't have to."

I shook my head. "I mean all of this."

"Okay—" He huffed. "Okay."

"I just want to go home." I finally shifted to look at him.

When he made eye contact, I recognized the disappointment and sorrow. He slowly nodded and looked away. "Maybe we can continue this conversation in the morning, yeah?"

"Yeah." I nodded, scanning the room, trying to piece together what led to all this.

"As of now, are you okay?" His voice was gentle, soothing.

"Peachy." I nodded, wiping a stray tear from my eye.

"Peachy cobbler?"

I shook my head, confused. "I can use a drink."

"That I can provide." He slid to the corner of the bed, but before he fully stood, a dark spot in the corner of the room grabbed my attention.

My eyes widened. "There. Look!" I pointed to the bar counter where I had sat earlier. "Something's there. You see it?"

Nolan stared but shook his head. "I don't see anything."

"It's a dark ... thing. A shadow." I grabbed my chest in horror. "Maybe it's her. That girl."

Nolan stood in all his naked glory, not concerned one bit with the darkening shadow. "Let me get you another drink. It'll relax you. Trust me." He dismissed my concern and headed toward the kitchen.

The shadow quickly manifested into a dark, opaque silhouette that darted across the room. Nolan paused, and I could have sworn his head darted in the phantom's direction as it zipped into the kitchen.

I only had a split second to comprehend what was happening before the silhouette darted to the wine bottle, knocking it off the counter. I flinched as the glass bottle hit the floor and shattered. Dark red liquid pooled where it landed.

"What in the bloody hell—" slipped out of Nolan's lips as a whisper.

So, I wasn't crazy. "You saw that, didn't you?"

He stared at the spot for a while, worrying me, and causing me to stand. I refused to go anywhere near the kitchen, Nolan, or the glass. I pulled the satin sheet from the bed and secured it around me more for comfort than modesty.

"I—how did?" He stuttered. "The wine."

"I told you I saw something." I pointed to the counter where the silhouette manifested. "It's a woman that looks just like me. I think she's haunting us. Maybe she's haunting this room or the entire studio."

"Rhea," Nolan finally turned to me, "take a deep breath. Calm down, alright?"

"But you saw it, didn't you?" I took a step forward. "You saw the shadow."

He shook his head. "No. I didn't see a shadow or a woman. What happened was the bottle fell off the counter." He ran his hand through his hair. "I must've placed it too close to the edge." He groaned in frustration. "Relax, Rhea. I'll clean it up. Cleaning up messes is my specialty."

**7**

CHAPTER 7

I didn't even recall falling asleep. I only remembered waking with a terrible headache pounding my temple and the remnants of the unexplained red wine stains on the pretty white tile of the kitchen floor.

I recalled witnessing the humanoid shadow rush across the room toward the wine bottle before it hit the floor, but much of what happened after became a blur. Thankful that I got some much-needed rest, I left Nolan furiously trying to scrub the stain from the tiles and entered the brightly lit studio. I noted his irritation and thought it best to slip out of the room without interrupting.

My curiosity led me to my computer at the lone desk in the corner of the massive, empty room. I secured the terrycloth robe around me and chuckled at the comically sized workspace compared to the room. It made sense why it was there, to keep our work professional, efficient and convenient. Plus, the perfect white backdrop was great for showcasing my wardrobe when live streaming. Despite that, I couldn't help but snort at the disproportionate setup.

Nolan's muffled voice could be heard from across the short distance between the rooms. From the sound of it, he was in a business meeting. I could tell by the clear, concise demeanor and the lack of curse words which he used while speaking to himself when picking up stray pieces of glass from the floor.

I went online to search for ghosts and hauntings. Anything that could explain what I was experiencing and why. I sought information that linked hauntings and headaches, the meaning of mirror phantoms, and the dangers of ghosts that closely resembled oneself. Nothing seemed helpful and a lot of the material contradicted each another, but I continued my online investigation because I'd become determine to find something, anything, that could help.

Mentions of salt, circles, candles, and crystals all seemed pointless in my logical mind. What I really wanted to know was why this was happening to me?

Being related to stress or even a brain injury was out of the question after Nolan seemed to see it and it interacted with our physical environment.

I continued to search as the single door across the studio opened to Joselyn and a tray of two iced coffees and one hot black in her hand.

"Rhea!" she squealed. "Look at you, beautiful. You ready for today's photo sesh?"

The door closed and automatically locked behind her, and she only continued to strut toward me, balancing the tray expertly in one hand and the keycard to unlock the door in the other. Her high heels click-clacked as usual, and her handbag dangled from the strap that was tucked in the crook of her elbow.

"Hey, Jos." I turned in my seat to receive the refreshing chilled drink. "This may sound so gross, but I haven't even showered yet."

"Still beautiful, even while stewing in your own filth." She chuckled. "Where's Nolan?"

"I think he's in a meeting in the other room." I nodded at his coffee. "You can just leave it here."

"Cool beans." She sat the tray down. "Don't we have makeup coming in less than an hour and a shoot to set up?"

"You would know." I nodded.

"Yes, I would know, and that's the case. So, get showered, beauty queen."

"I'm just a little reluctant to use that bathroom," I admitted. "Last night, the craziest thing happened. I swear I saw that ghost woman in the mirror."

"Oh, my god." She pulled her coffee straw from her lips. "Are you serious?"

"Seriously." I nodded. "And later a shadow rushed across the room and knocks down a bottle of wine from the counter. Wine and glass everywhere." I mimicked the shattered glass by throwing my arms up, fingers spread.

Her eyes widened, enough to see the whites fully around the blues. "You're shitting me!"

"I wish I was." I sighed, still trying to process what I had witnessed.

She dipped an eyebrow, refusing to take her eyes from me as if scrutinizing. "What does Nolan think about it?"

"He saw it too." I nodded. My eyes went just as wide as hers.

"You're double shitting me." She gasped, bringing her hand up to her throat in shock. "This studio is freaking haunted? Holy hell."

"It's crazy, but I literally freaked out." I massaged my temples, trying to push down all the elevated feelings coming to the surface. "I want to get out of here."

She occupied her hand by tossing her long blond tresses into a tight ponytail. "But what about the shoot and your other obligations?"

"Fuck 'em." I shrugged.

Although she stood stationary, she kept active by using her hands. This time, she fidgeted with the straw of her drink and smacked her lips after taking a sip. "Stop it. You're too professional to leave your sponsors and fans hanging."

She was right, but since seeing that eerie woman, I haven't been comfortable in this space. "A day here is enough."

"Well, you only have one more day to go." She nodded to encourage me. "You can do it. Also, I added an early morning appointment with your doctor to the calendar."

Business as usual. "Thanks," I said dryly.

The sound of Nolan still speaking on the phone cut through the brief silence.

"How are you guys doing?" Joselyn nudged toward the sound of his voice.

"Why?" I sneered curiously. Could she tell things were not as they used to be? Was there an awkwardness in the air that she picked up on?

"I don't know," she shrugged. "You guys seem a little ... off."

A hollow pit in my stomach formed at the mention. She was right. Things were off and now her mentioning it let me know that our private troubles weren't so private or subtle. But how much should I reveal to her if anything? "Yesterday wasn't the best."

"Oh, no." She sat her cup down, giving me her utmost attention. "What happened?"

"I don't really remember what triggered him, but when I asked for my phone, he threw it and it hit me. Really hard." Just remembering the moment made a pit form in my gut. It was as if it had happened moments ago and felt like the incident had refused me time to sleep off the impact of it.

"Oh, shit." Her voice lowered, growing more concerned. "Are you okay?"

I shook my head. "Physically, yes. Emotionally?" I refused eye contact. I couldn't bear to see the judgement in her eyes.

"Was it an accident?" Her low voice came out like a whisper and held a genuine interest.

I dipped my head to avoid looking at her, but my heart told me to speak the truth despite the embarrassment I tried so desperately to avoid. "He apologized after, but I think he did it on purpose. To hurt me."

"At least he apologized." She picked up her cup and continued to sip. "I mean, you both are freaking out over this enormous opportunity. I mean, Rhea, you're like the most highly anticipated online star walking the catwalk during the biggest fashion event ever. That's a lot of pressure on you and anyone calling themselves your manager."

I finally looked up, taken aback by her cavalier attitude. "He hurt me, Jos." I searched her eyes for a hint of sympathy.

"I'm sure he didn't mean it." She rubbed my shoulder in a half-ass attempt to comfort me. "He's managing tons of people and re-sponsibilities, and it can get really chaotic trying to hold everything together."

My fingers nervously tapped the desktop, and I narrowed my eyes at her response. "What do you mean, he's managing other people? I'm his only client."

"Oops." Her chuckle came out stifled from nervousness. "It was supposed to be a surprise. I'm sorry." The nervousness on her face didn't last long as she quickly tried to straighten up.

I questioned her with my eyes before the words even came out of my mouth. "What's going on?"

She looked over her shoulder and whispered, "You remember I told you I am looking to move to Cali and break into acting?"

"You said that was a dream." I looked toward the room I had left Nolan in and quickly debated what to do if he appeared.

"It is! And Nolan offered to manage me." The excitement in her voice made her confession come out in a low squeal. "He said he wanted to surprise you with the news but after the fashion event, because he didn't want to interfere with your plans." Suddenly, she took on the demeanor of someone with their hand caught in the cookie jar. "But just don't tell him I told you yet. Okay?"

Wow. Secrets.

I nearly shook my head in disbelief, scoffing inside at her admission, but I didn't respond. I only tried my best to not react, but a considerable part of me was pissed and a bit hurt. No, betrayed. What else had Nolan been keeping from me?

The feeling of being out of the loop and deceived by someone I trusted took me back to a time I had wanted to forget. "You know I used to get bullied in high school by a guy on the football team?"

She removed the straw from her lips before frowning. "Aw. That sucks."

"The worse part was my mom used to say he was only picking on me because he liked me. And I convinced myself that him pushing me against the locker and calling me a bitch every day was because he had a crush. It didn't matter that he already had a girlfriend or flirted with other girls without pushing them against trash cans. The entire thing had convinced Mom that his behavior was all for love."

"Wow. That really sucks, Rhea." She dropped her gaze, finally putting her iced coffee on the desk. "You know, I never had the chance to meet your mom."

"We stopped talking after I realized we didn't understand each other. She's so stuck in her ways, a in a different time. And here I am, in reality. We could never see eye to eye about anything, my relationships, my career, nothing."

"Sounds like a screwy mess."

"Tell me about it." I shook my head. "Worse part, a few years ago, she would schedule a date and time to come see me and I would set an alarm on my phone to remind me. The worse thing ever was to hear that alarm go off for days in a row and yet she'd never make it. She had more excuses than my deadbeat dad. After a while, I just stopped all communication."

"Maybe one day you'd see the alarms you set weren't for nothing." She lifted an eyebrow and gave a slight nod.

"That's my point. I'm always forgiving. I'm always giving second and third chances to people who keep hurting me—" I stopped myself before I went on an uncontrollable emotional tirade, but the impulse was there.

I'd often wonder if my time was better spent venting to a therapist rather than holding it all in. At least a professional could help me figure out ways to work through the issue or even find a great way to cope if working through it proved unsuccessful.

She nodded, seeming to become restless. "I know it sucks, but I'm gonna deliver this coffee to Nolan before it gets cold."

I gulped down my frustration and nodded, watching her walk away with the tray containing a single cup of hot black coffee in one hand and her iced coffee in the other.

It was after she disappeared into the hall that I realized I had been tapping my fingers in a rhythm that matched an annoying ad on the computer. The loud, rhythmic beeping caught my attention as the words instructed me to "run, don't walk" to the nearest pest control company before a special deal was over. I placed my fidgeting hands in my lap and stared suspiciously at the rest of the pest control commercial as it played in a banner at the bottom of my screen.

**8**

CHAPTER 8

The photoshoot went on for hours with makeup touchups, lunch and breaks in between. I was thankful my Sunday consisted of so many duties that took my mind off the things I wanted to forget.

Nolan had been emotionally distant most of the day, putting himself in manager mode as he took care of business arrangements. Joselyn brought lunch and snacks, helped schedule obligations, and I was sure some of those preparations and calls were for her and her budding acting career they were secretly working on.

Before I knew it, the day was nearly over.

Joselyn gave me a quick goodbye hug before leaving the building for the evening, leaving Nolan and I alone in the large studio and attached apartment. The perfect time to talk.

Nolan removed his tailored dark blue blazer and tossed it on the edge of the bed. "What a day, yeah?" He sighed, releasing a bit of stress, and relaxing his broad shoulders. "Come, you sexy vixen." He crooked a finger and produced those deep cheek dimples with a smile.

"We haven't had a chance to really talk about last night," I started, making my way to him as if being pulled by a magnet or maybe habit.

"That's because there's nothing to talk about." His eyelids were low, he looked more tired than aroused as I had assumed. "You had a good time, didn't you?"

"Honestly, it's all a bit of a blur." I stood before him, hesitant to fall into his arms like my body wanted to. "But that wine—"

"It was too close to the edge. Nothing else." His fingertips caressed my jawline. "You're too sexy to worry about shattered wine bottles." He guided me closer so his lips could press against mine.

I didn't close my eyes like he did.

When he pulled back, his palms slid down my side, but I ignored his blatant gesture. "We never talked about what happened before the wine." I looked into his disappointed eyes and refused to look away. "You hurt me, Nolan."

"Hurting you was a mistake I made up for by making you scream my name in pleasure."

I scoffed. "Are you serious?"

"Rhea Patel ..." he started and rubbed his nose in annoyance.

"Nolan Hudson," I mimicked.

"We're better now," he insisted. "Why rewind time just to relive the pain? Let's move on, yeah?"

"Sure." I dropped my head in defeat. If only I had the courage to walk right out of the building and never look back. The security of my future and the fearful unknown were the only things stopping me.

He lifted his phone. "I'm gonna respond to some emails and then climb into bed to get some shuteye before dinner. How does that sound?"

I nodded and left him alone in the room. The emails could have very well been opportunities for Joselyn and her career that he didn't want me to intrude on. And being so exhausted put me in a mood where arguing wasn't welcomed.

Back in the studio, the bright lights were disorienting as I was sure the sun had set, but the lack of windows made it difficult to know what time of day it was without looking at the time. Even so, I was thankful for the lights as it kept all the darkness at bay.

I made my way across the room to sit at the desk.

Upon sitting, I replayed the morning events in my head especially the conversation with Joselyn. The mention of my mother and our estranged relationship came to mind, and I couldn't help but wonder if a link between the eerie woman and Mom existed? I picked up my phone and without hesitation selected her contact info. When the phone rang and rang, the worry began to set in.

Suddenly the ringing stopped, and Mom's familiar voice answered, "Rhea?"

I hung up.

I waited for a few minutes with the phone resting in my shaky palm to see if she'd return the call. Just like her promises to visit, she never did, but at least she was okay, so my worry meter quickly decreased.

I listened to the sound of silence that hummed throughout the space. Not even the sound of Nolan talking to himself could be heard. Him sleeping was equivalent to me being left by myself, and the thought of being alone didn't ease my nerves the way I had hoped. I put the phone down and logged into my UpTube account. I knew just what could help me keep my mind from the things that worried me.

I hit start on a livestream and quickly watched the number of dedicated fans rise. Their excited comments brought a smile to my face.

"Hey, guys!" I waved at the computer, keeping my eyes focused on the little camera lens and the green pinprick of light in the top center of the screen. "Thought it would be a good time to talk to you all. I had a busy day of photoshoots and spent hours doing two different makeup looks. You like?" I puckered my lips to the heart emojis in the comments.

"I have to keep it down because Nolan is sleeping right now, but how have you guys been?"

Comments rolled in  asking what happened during the last livestream and why I abruptly disappeared without explanation.

"We missed you! Where did you go? Yay, Rhea and Nolan forever. We stan Rhelan! Why did you cut the last stream?"

I knew better than to bring the fans into my personal issues but being open about some things appealed to me. And what would be a better time to express myself than while Nolan was sleeping?

"I know I left without saying goodbye last time, part of it is because it's a super busy time right now. As you all know, fashion week begins tomorrow, and although I'm super excited, I'm super stressed too," I started, taking a moment to convince myself honesty was the best course of action. Truthfully, learning of Nolan's plan to manage Joselyn and him keeping it a secret didn't sit well with me. I something told me I wouldn't have another chance to bear my true feelings and concerns. Maybe getting it off my chest publicly was the best way to be heard. "I think I convinced myself that I could handle anything and everything that comes my way, but I'm not sure that's the case.

"For a moment, I lost track of what's important to me and now all I want is to break free of the things holding me back or tying me down. Just like my sponsorship with Salty Saddles Leggings, the controversy behind their business practices is something I never wanted to be associated with. But I'm the one making business decisions."

A dark spot in the far corner of the pristine white room caught my eye and my heart skipped a beat. I gulped, watching the darkness grow and expand. I kept my eye on the developing form and took a steady breath, keeping my fear in check. I told myself to keep talking to the camera and not to react.

"I should've been honest with you all long before fashion week, but the truth is I wasn't aware that I would be the new face of SSL until I was notified by my manager."

The camera continued to record, the numbers of live viewers steadily rose, and the dark shadow across the room gradually formed into the familiar slender silhouette of the red-haired woman I recognized every time I peered at my reflection.

She wore my exact same outfit, the dark teal SSL athletic leggings and matching tank top. The only thing that differentiated us was our hairstyles, mine was in a sloppy ponytail to keep the strands from obstructing my view. Her deep red hair floated about her head as if she were submerged in a body of water, but still I couldn't place my finger on why the shape of her head disturbed me more than her transparent outline.

As I told myself to keep talking and keep the fans on the live to increase my sense of security, my give-a-care meter continued to drop. "I've been so stressed lately that I swear I'm seeing things that would make me seem crazy if I didn't think others didn't see them too."

I refused to gauge the viewers reaction by tearing my gaze from the fully formed woman standing directly before me. Only the outline of her wasn't as solid as I would expect from a real person standing only feet away.

"I don't know what I should do, but I know I need things to change."

Nervousness took over my body as I anticipated something wicked about to happen. A sense of dread caused my fingertips to rhythmically tap against the surface of the desk. I only noticed when her fingers mimicked mine, tap, tap, tap on her thigh.

My eyes widened when I realized she wasn't only copying me, but her drumming fingers matched perfectly with my own. I couldn't make out the emotion conveyed on her face as her facial features looked off.

But when my fingers stopped, so did hers.

When I cocked my head in confusion, she did too. What was happening? Curiosity overpowered my fear, and I knew now was the time for answers.

"I'll talk to you all about it more later. For now, I have to let you go." I ended the stream and watched the woman. Although on edge and anxious, I no longer felt threatened by her.

"Who are you?" I murmured to myself.

The lids around her eyes widened although her face was difficult to see. Blurred and distorted, only the colors of her lips and the shadow of her nose allowed me to fill in the blanks with my imagination. She lifted her arm to point to me.

I pressed my forefinger into my chest, trying to understand what she was trying to communicate. Then I realized she must've been pointing at the computer in front of me. I stared at the screen to see the commercial from earlier. Although the sound had been muted, the words "Run don't walk" stood out.

My heart sank.

"Are you trying to tell me something?" I finally asked, the adrenaline surging through my body nearly caused me to panic. My breathing became so rapid I knew at any moment I would hyperventilate. "Is this a warning?"

I stood in preparation of what was to come.

Her jaw dropped and her mouth opened as she pointed again, this time behind me. I turned to see Nolan shaking his head.

"What is going on with you?" His voice came out in a chilling whisper. "First, you wreck both of our careers on UpTube Live, and now you're talking to a wall?"

"What?" I turned back to the woman who was no longer there. In fact, only the white wall stood in her place. "I—I—"

"You're ill, Rhea." He shook his head again. "And now I must figure out what to do about that."

**9**

**CHAPTER 9**

I couldn't explain what I had seen and trying to would be pointless when Nolan believed everything that had happened came about due to a sickness. I stared at his mouth as we stood in the corner of the brightly lit studio.

"You're utterly insane to say what you said on a public platform." It was obvious he hadn't been sleeping at all as he was still fully clothed in his button-down long sleeve shirt and navy slacks. Even his expensive dress shoes were still secured to his feet. "I saw it all. Apparently, you never wanted to be the spokesperson for SSL? Well, that's news to me, especially since you signed the contract. Ms. Rhea Patel."

"No, I didn't like how they implied only certain types of people could wear their clothes." I raised my voice as he had, releasing my unbridled frustrations. "I told you that, and you, yes you, Mr. Nolan Hudson, convinced me to sign the contract because it was 'a great financial move.' So, thank you for convincing me to sell my soul."

He chuckled. "So, now I forced your signature on that contract?"

"I had morals." I sneered in disgust.

"What is morality when there's money involved?" He scoffed and stuffed his hands in his pant pockets.

I shook my head, taking in his cold demeanor. "You don't care about me. This whole relationship is based on padding your pockets. Just admit it."

"How dare you say that!" He narrowed his eyes, finally showing a heart by placing his hand above his. "It's clear you have no idea how much I love you. Sure, the money is great, but I will literally lay down and die for you. After all these years, how can you not see it?"

"You say that every time I threaten to leave and live my life the way I want," I shook my head, forcing myself not to believe it this time. "That's always been your way of making me feel guilty, so I stay, and we make love, and the cycle continues. But not anymore, Nolan. It ends today."

"Rhea, come on now." He gulped then sighed. "Listen—"

"No, I'm always listening. That's all I do, but when is it my turn to start being listened to?" I shook my head. "If you really loved me or cared, you would've told me you wanted to manage Joselyn Murphy's acting career. But you didn't because that's a conflict of interest and you know I wouldn't have agreed."

"So, she told you, huh?" He dropped his gaze. "This is what this is about, me managing Joselyn? I didn't want to upset you during fashion week, but I couldn't pass up the opportunity. An old producer buddy is working on his debut film and needed a female lead. So—"

"I don't care." I swiped the air with my hand dismissively. "As of now, you're no longer my manager or my man. You can do as you please." I took a step in an attempt to leave the space.

"Rhea, you're not thinking this through." His voice grew an octave, causing me to stop in my tracks. "You need me. This is an important week. This week is everything. Are you just going to throw that away?"

"You know, I had convinced myself that this career path was becoming too much for me and that fashion and the spotlight was a mistake, but I now realize that my mistake was being with you." I shook my head and scoffed at the egotistical man before me. "You're the problem and you've always been."

"Don't say that." His voice came out in a strained whisper, his shoulders slumped, and I realized there had been a frail and powerless man beneath that egotistical veneer all along. "Please, Rhea. You're all I have. You're all I live for. Everything I've ever done, including agreeing to manage Joselyn, was for you."

Even though him looking so distraught was a first, I have heard those words plenty of times before. And this time they didn't affect me the way they had then.

I picked up the cell phone on the edge of the desk. "I'm calling my mom and telling her I'm finally coming home, because I'm not staying here one more night."

"Are you serious?" His eyebrows dipped and his abrupt anger caused his voice to come out aggressively. "You'd reconcile with that woman after the things she's said about you, us, and your career? She wished ill on you for choosing the path you chose."

"I'm sure she'd be forgiving knowing I'm choosing a different one now." I brought up her contact info, but the phone was swiped from my grip before I could dial. "Give me my phone, Nolan." I put my hand out, demanding what belonged to me.

"I can't let you make that mistake." He slid it into his pant pocket. "You'll thank me later. Trust me."

I knew this routine, and I refused to go down that path again. I rolled my eyes, shook my head, and made my way to the adjacent apartment to gather my stuff. "I can't believe you're doing this."

He followed. "You know I know what's best for you. Have I steered you wrong yet?"

I refused to entertain him or his theories and searched for my shoes. "So ridiculous," I murmured to myself.

"Where are you going?" He stood near the bar counter and crossed his arms over his chest. "You're seriously not leaving. It's late and dark out there, Rhea. You can't go anywhere by yourself. Crazed fans exist, you know?"

I crossed my arms like he did. "So, what are you gonna do? Hold me hostage?"

"I intend to protect you," he said matter-of-factly. "That's my job. That's what you hired me to do."

"I hired you as a manager to manage my career and I trusted you as a boyfriend to love me like I deserve, and now because you failed at both, you're fired." Finally, the power I knew I always had surged through me, and it felt good to say what I'd been feeling for so long. "You, Mr. Nolan Hudson, are fired from ever again being associated with Rhea Patel or her likeness."

He pinched the bridge of his nose and sniffed.

I lost my patience long ago and couldn't afford to pretend to care. I spotted my shoes, grabbed them, and sat on the sofa to put them on.

"Four years down the drain? Just like that?" His voice trembled as he tried to control his emotions.

"This goodbye was long overdue." I secured my shoelaces and retrieved my purse which contained a copy of the car key.

"My parents disappeared from my life the same way you're leaving now, grabbed their car keys and walked right out of the door, never looking back." When he looked up, his eyes glistened and the deep dimples on his cheeks that used to turn me on were now only vessels to collect his tears. "They left me because I chose you and your passions, because you are more important to me than anything. I thought I had proved that. Look at the life you have."

"I'm sorry, Nolan." I sighed. "I truly am sorry. You were there for me. You taught me a lot, especially how to become the well-spoken professional I am today. I'll give you that. But all good things must come to an end."

"You never cared about me," he sneered. "Not like I cared for you."

"I've been seeing a creepy woman since we got here and you tell me I'm sick and I'm stressed, but you won't allow me to see a doctor or take a break. If I'm having a mental breakdown, a caring person would get me help and not push me to keep performing."

"I'm looking out for your career." His frustration came through as he growled through clenched teeth.

"Fine, I get it. You were doing your job, but now you're released from that responsibility." I ignored his penetrating glare. "It's over, Nolan." I pushed past him heading toward the door, but before I could take another step I was pulled back by my ponytail.

"You're not going anywhere," he snarled.

I yelped and instinct urged me to grip his hands to pull them from my hair. "What are you doing? Stop, Nolan. Let me go."

"I can't do that."

His tug caught me off balance and I hit the floor, falling back on my ass. My hair brushed my shoulders as it fell from the ponytail. When I looked up, the elastic tie along with a good chunk of my hair projected from his fist.

I screamed, not from pain but from the terror of what would come next. I managed to get to my feet, but the sight of my eerie double and the frightened look on her face startled me. Seeing her up close, the dent in the side of her head near the temple, the fear in her wide eyes and the trail of blood that pooled beneath them.

Her mouth formed the word "no," but her stare locked onto what was happening behind me. I turned just as the heavy, diamond shaped multicultural award left Nolan's hands to impact my temple.

I went down like a feather, staring up at the man that called me his everything and the look of fear and instant regret on his face as the award clanked to the ground beside me.

The urge to turn and examine the splatters of blood took over me, but I couldn't move. Fear paralyzed me, or something else did. I wanted to cry, I thought I was, but I couldn't feel the hot tears running down my face.

What was happening?

"Oh, fuck," Nolan whispered through trembling lips. "What have I done? Rhea, baby?"

In my peripheral vision, the strands of my hair fanned out around my head like a flaming red halo in contrast to the darkness creeping in.

What did you do, Nolan? How could you?

I tried to respond but my mouth didn't move, and blackness crept in much like my fear, swallowing me whole. From the utter obscurity, the distant sound of a familiar male voice echoed, prompting me, urging me, persuading me.

"Eyes wide open."

**10**

**CHAPTER 10**

I blinked and only blackness surrounded me. A feeling of surrealism encompassed me, like floating in an open space without boundaries. Yet my fingertips grazed solid ground, then my palm registered the cold tiles beneath me and pressed at my back. Only then I realized I had been lying on the floor. I pushed myself up, amazed but petrified at the utter confusion of it all.

I managed to get to my feet, an unsteadiness washed over me making me woozy. My eyes scanned the space and my surroundings for even a pinprick of light. Although a sweeping coldness made the area seem massive and never-ending, the utter darkness triggered my claustrophobia.

Soon, I would panic and hyperventilate, and I tried to combat that anxiety and prevent the loss of my sanity by finding a light source. In the distance, a tiniest of brightness caught my eye. And like a magnet, it drew me in. I moved toward the light steadily as if I were floating, yet the ground beneath my feet was the only solid thing around.

I tried looking ahead to make sure I wouldn't walk off an edge and fall into a crevice, but the darkness forced me to trust the ground would remain firm beneath me.

The light grew larger the closer I got and soon the lit room came into perfect view. Standing at the threshold of the bright room, I took in a medical bed with white railings. The bed rested in the center with a pristine tile floor and white walls that reminded me of the photography studio, yet the machinery attached to the person lying motionless in the bed reminded me of my last visit to a hospital where I had tubes in me measuring my blood pressure and oxygen.

The astringent smell of medicine entered my nostrils, further establishing I was indeed in a hospital room. That harsh smell was a reason I hated visiting hospitals, but this time I had no choice judging by what I saw.

The red-haired woman in the bed was me. She lay on her back, although her eyes were closed her bandaged head rested to the side facing me. The outline of her petite upper body and bronze skin of her arms that peeked from the white sheet was just as wispy as the doppelganger had been, prompting me to look down over myself to compare.

My own body seemed solid and not translucent as the women in bed. My heartbeat still raced through my body, causing it to thump with every rapid beat as I tried to figure out what was happening to me.

Was I dead?

I studied the bloodied bandage around the women's head and the machines monitoring her vitals and the realization hit me. That woman is me but why was I here observing her?

The tube going into her nose must've given her oxygen or liquid nutrients, I couldn't tell, but it didn't look right or comfortable. My heart sank at the condition she was in, but I still couldn't understand why she was there, and I was here.

I looked past her to the nothingness behind her. It was only when I focused on that emptiness, that more of the scene manifested. Dozens of posters, stuffed animals, and handwritten letters littered the room.

Drawings of Nolan and I with embracing caught my attention more than the others. Notes instructing me to wake up. Letters wishing me well. Prayers from fans from every area of the globe, judging by the variety of languages on the items.

One beautiful painting confused me as it depicted Nolan wrapping me in large wings that protruded from his back like an angel with the hashtag #RhelanForever written on his wing.

I shook my head, confused.

Nolan did this to me. He did that to her, putting that woman in the hospital. Didn't the fans or anyone know that? Why would they depict him as some sort of guardian angel? And why would they draw him with wings and not the other way around?

I tried to determine what I was looking at and why I was observing it. Was this a glimpse of the past, present, or future? Was I dreaming? Was all this a hallucination as a result of my injuries?

My mind flooded with confusion and as I tried to approach the woman in bed, the brightly lit area moved as I did, keeping me from stepping into the room. I wanted to touch her, to see if I could feel her warmth and determine she was alive or even real at all, but the more I tried to enter the space the more it moved further from me.

Out of frustration I pressed my hands to my head. What was happening?

The wet stickiness of blood from my temple marked my palm when I removed it. I stared at the spot reliving the moment that caused it.

The look in Nolan's eyes, the anger in his tone, the hatred in his actions. How could he do this to me?

I swiped my hand through my hair to examine the extent of the wound, feeling a large indentation in my skull. I gasped and pulled my hand away and waited until my courage had been restored to try it again.

I gently pressed my fingers to my scalp again, and although my head didn't feel normal there was no pain which I appreciated. Still, my hair seemed to float around me as if gravity didn't exist, and no matter how much I tried to slick it down and back it remained as if it had a mind of its own.

A sudden sound from far behind me took my attention and I pivoted to examine the distant click, click, click that chimed like the steady rhythm of a second hand as it moved around the face of a clock.

I stared into the blackness and the clicks became louder as if fast approaching, the closer it got the more familiar the sound became. A camera in action.

I glanced back to the hospital scene but was encompassed in blackness. I drew in a sharp breath of cold air as it hit me that the brightly lit room had disappeared. I turned back to clicking camera sounds, hoping to see the camera that caused it.

Yet the echoey sound of Nolan's instruction cut through the camera sounds. "Eyes wide open."

I stared ahead at the scene unfolding before my very eyes. The bright light prompted me to move forward to get a better look at another version of me standing before the camera topless in a pair of SSL yoga pants.

"Extend your elbow and arch your back," Nolan encouraged, his cheery British accent breaking through his acquired American one.

I watched as Joselyn captured the last of the shots and exited the room with the camera in hand. My eyes widened as I recognized this moment. I predicted what was to happen next by replaying the events in my memory while watching it play out before me.

"What's going on in that pretty little head of yours?" Nolan winked as he placed a terrycloth robe around the other Rhea's naked shoulders. "You seem a bit off today."

"Nope." She flashed a smile, and I could see the bullshit in her vacant eyes. "Everything's peachy."

"Peachy cobbler?" He raised an eyebrow, and I hated how attractive he looked at that moment. I hated that I had allow his charm and good looks to suck me in and keep me stuck for so long.

"Peachy cobbler," she lied.

I knew he would direct that Rhea to sit down at the laptop and summon Joselyn to show her how beautiful she was with a snap of his fingers.

While I anticipated the click-clack of Joselyn's high heels on the tile floors, I tapped my fingers on my knee. The rhythmic beat from the pads of my fingers kept me from losing my sanity as I tried to piece together what was happening and why. I had to keep it together.

I watched the scene as she finally approached with the camera, excitedly willing to show that Rhea the beautiful shots she had taken at Nolan's request.

"Oh yay! Pics." Joselyn crouched down before that Rhea as she sat at the desk, angling the camera for her to see the screen. But the other Rhea wasn't looking at the pictures or the camera, her eyes seemed to land on me!

I stood wide-eyed and paralyzed, realizing the moment. Realizing the facts. Realizing that I had just gone back in time and was indeed reliving the moment where I had seen the wispy, shadowy humanoid figure in the corner of the brightly lit studio.

But this time, the wispy, shadowy figure was me.

I gasped just as the camera crashed to the floor after the other Rhea jumped to stand and accidentally knocked it from Joselyn's grip.

## 11

## CHAPTER 11

Watching the camera crash to the ground, bumped from Joselyn's hands, brought back the memory that eerily played out before my very eyes. That Rhea stood next to the desk in the corner, a terrycloth robe around her naked shoulders, Nolan, and Jos beside her. They each stared in my direction, but no one made eye contact or reacted the way I thought they would if they saw me.

The most important question hounded me. Why was I observing this scene and being forced to relive it? It was the exact same event as before, but now I was seeing it from a different perspective.

Was there something I could do to stop or change what had already happened? How would that be possible? Judging my surroundings made it difficult to decipher if I had been given a blessing or a curse.

Confused, I cocked my head, witnessing what I always suspected but never quite known until now. As Nolan wrapped his arms around that Rhea to comfort her, his eyes were indeed locked onto Jos's swaying hips as she click-clacked her way out of the studio.

Was that why time had rewound and brought me to the start of the weekend, to show me what a douche Nolan had been? The effort was pointless as I was more than familiar with his evil ways. What other reason was there to have me witness these instants? There was no need to push me back to these moments. Since the strike of the phone to my gut, I knew I should've left him. And even all the little cruel incidents before had made me questioned why I hadn't.

I knew now. I allowed his manipulation to hold me hostage, unwillingly letting his control seep in and convince me to act against my best interest. That had to be the reason. Or at least one of them. I knew better now, so what was the point of this? What was the point of making me watch these acts again?

The scene before me slowly faded into blackness at the thought, leaving me surrounded in a dark emptiness. Although I couldn't see much, the feeling of existing in a never-ending open space enveloped me.

Was this place Heaven, Hell, or something in between?

None of my questions were being answered, and a fear of being watched caused my skin to crawl. The sensation of my hair literally standing on end came over me like an ethereal mermaid in the stagnant waters of time. No matter how much I tried to get my hair to fall, the lack of gravity in the place kept it splayed around my head like the injured, lifeless Rhea Nolan left blooded on the floor.

I could see it now, the life slowly leaving her eyes while the long, red waves of her locks fanned out around her head like a crown of fire. Only to spread with the trail of blood that extended out like tenacles of an underwater sea creature. I didn't like that image, and I shook my head to erase it from my mind.

I gazed around the space, searching for and awaiting whatever approached. The soles of my shoes grazed the solid ground but there was no doubt that my body was floating. A sensation I wasn't sure I could get used to, but was surprised that somehow I maneuvered through it. The quietness of the space should have been nice, warm, and welcoming. Instead, a sense of dread swept over me, jostling my fears, awakening a sense of unease that I couldn't shake. A mysterious presence caused my skin to prickle with its energy and I turned to confront what stood behind me.

A thin feminine shape contrasted against the blackness. Long, wavy hair lay below her shoulders, falling like curtains. My eyes adjusted to the red hue of the strands, and I recognized her instantly. Her five-eight frame reminded me of Mom, familiar, especially the broad shoulders and slender hips...

A wave of déjà vu washed over me.

The more I stared, the more uneasy I became. She looked at me as if studying my features. And I felt myself getting closer, moving so slow, nearly floating. I tilted my head, questioning the scene and remembering the long, mysterious nap I had taken. I had dreamed of this moment. I remembered it clearly but viewing it from this perspective made me wonder. Was I the intruder of her dreams?

Her eyes never left me. I blamed curiosity for keeping them locked onto me, and I tried to remember my thoughts during that surreal dream. If this moment taught me anything, it was that what I had experienced during that long nap had not been a silly old nightmare.

Somehow, it was happening ... now.

It reminded me of the books I read in high school about the famous psychologist Carl Jung. Being assigned to write a report on his theories of dreams led me to becoming a fan of his philosophies, and I couldn't get enough. I had always assumed my psyche had been communicating important things I couldn't grasp. Things about my associations and relationships, and my interpretation of love.

If I had somehow gone back in time and was given the chance to communicate with my past self, now was my chance to deliver a very important message. The only thing that Rhea needed to know.

For a split second, she dropped her gaze, and the outline of her silhouette began to blend with the ethereal bluish-black background. Soon, she would disappear before my very eyes. I knew she would and expected it. Much like a phantom, she would vanish. I rushed forward to demand her attention, bringing an icy wind that nearly stopped my heart. "Run!"

Her eyes widened and like a snap of a finger, she was gone. Only the twisting and twirling mist of the air stood before me.

Before I could properly react to her sudden disappearance, a voice ahead stopped me cold. "Ah, baby. I missed you." The murky atmosphere carried the male voice like a hollow echo from the distance, the slight British accent stopped my heart. "I knew I would find you, Rhea. I knew we would meet again."

I stumbled back, subconsciously pulling away from the voice and the person who owned it. I could make out the murky silhouette in the distance. An even darker, human shaped void against the backdrop of the blackish-blue space. I anticipated what would happen when he got close enough, imagining all the varied scenarios in my mind.

The urge to turn and run came over me but I didn't, knowing there was nowhere to go. Much like my career and romantic relationship. Throughout the growth of both, I struggled with the duality of wanting to leave, to call it quits. But every time I'd get so close to doing just that, Nolan would convince me otherwise.

He would so often persuade me with his charm, his threats, and his manipulation. I haven't been so happy for so long and yet I stayed. I had stayed and dealt with the lies, the control, the isolation. I had stayed through the pain and unhappiness, and it only led me to this.

Leaving should have been the decision I came to for myself. Walking away should have been something I decided to do on my own. I was upset with myself seeing that the only way to break that habit and leave this relationship was for him to kill me.

My eyes locked onto Nolan's figure far in the distance that stood in the form of a shadow. His voice cut through the eerie darkness and haze, reaching my ears like a faint whisper. "You will never leave me. I will always find you."

I backed away. Although I felt light on my feet, the solid ground beneath my steps kept me grounded.

What was Nolan doing here? Why couldn't he just let me be? Wasn't it enough that he had hurt me, bashed my head in, killed me? What more could he want from me?

I gave up my family for him. I gave over my career. I put his needs and wants before my very own, giving him all of me. For so long, he had been in control and even now he wouldn't let go of that domination. Every cell of flesh and blood. He took all that from me with one blow. Why couldn't he just let me go? Wasn't that enough?

As I stood in the massive space, I focused on his distant footsteps approaching from ahead. The steps didn't sound like the familiar and rhythmic clunk, clunk, clunk, but a slight scraping and dragging that increase slightly as he approached. I match his steps with my own, moving backwards to keep a safe distance between us. I had no intention of letting him find me, and my confidence rose, believing the darkness was on my side.

"I know you're here, Rhea." His voice ricocheted from the misty particles that moved around us like smoke in a dark shade of blue. "I know that scent anywhere. Ah, how much I missed you, baby."

My bottom lip trembled at the thought of him finding me. What would he do if he did? What kind of pain and shock could I endure that could be worse than what he had already done to me? Hot tears blurred my vision and I squeezed from everywhere to prevent myself from whimpering. I thought about holding my breath, afraid that he could zone in on my breathing although I wasn't sure if I even was.

I continued to step back, but the sound of his quick approaching footsteps forced me to turn and run. Like a dirty trick, I ran smack into an object, and the force knocked me to my ass. I gasped as I looked up to see the object I had ran into. There he was as the emaciated figure before me.

Nolan stood there, his toes pointed as if he were hovering and only his toes grazed the ground. His pale, gaunt face frightened me more than his presence. He looked nothing like the man I had fallen in love with and repeatedly made love to. This man was far from handsome in this form. And when he lifted his arms to reach for me, a fresh stream of bright red blood painted his pale forearms.

Even if I wanted to hold onto my scream, I would have lost that battle. As a shriek escaped me, it tore from my vocal cords, leaving my throat sore and singed with a burning heat.

"Rhea..." Nolan's mouth didn't move as he spoke, but I heard him as clear as ever. "I knew I'd find you. It's you and me forever, baby."

**12**

**CHAPTER 12**

Running in the space felt more surreal than a dream. I never knew which direction I was headed, or where I'd end up, but I aimed to get far away from eerie Nolan as I could. Fear dove me to move as fast as my feet would carry to make distance between us.

But the ethereal fog rushed in, leaving me in the open space that suffocated me in darkness.

Up ahead through the mist stood a mirror in the nothingness. As I approached, I took in the sights of what was reflected to me in the glass. The big beautiful red hair surrounding my head drew me in and my eyes couldn't turn away. I moved closer, not walking but hovering as if the ground beneath me disappeared and only air push me through the space.

The image within the smooth clean glass displayed what was behind me as I realized the mirror allowed me to see through the blackness of the surrounding space. As I glared at my image in the mirror a sensation came over me.

The realization that I was not alone or as safe as I had hope filled my mind. I knew any moment the eerie, gaunt ghostly version of Nolan could appear out of thin air and attack, but the mirror called to me. My attention was solely on what it revealed. The girl who looked back seemed scared and lonely. The hollowness around her eyes made me feel sorry for the hell she experienced.

I stared, hoping she would stare back but she didn't. She never took interest in seeing herself, afraid of confronting the truth she tried to escape. The truth about how happy she really was had always been her weaknesses, one she couldn't bear to face.

"You're stronger than this," I told the girl in the mirror. "You're smarter than this. You deserve better than this. What are you doing? Why do you keep believing his lies?" As the words left my lips, I was surprised to see my reflection turn away.

Before I could grab her attention with my cries and demands, she turned the faucet on and cupped her hands under the flowing water. With her hand, she splashed water over the mirror, distorting the image into a smeared faced figure.

When she finally made eye contact, our eyes locked, and she knew that the woman who looked back was not only her reflection. She knew we were one. And I couldn't let this moment pass. This was my chance to stop her, to save her, to keep her from going back to Nolan and falling into his arms. In my excitement, I pressed my palms to the glass, hoping she'd know that I was real and take me seriously.

Instead, her eyes widened with fear. Shock was written all over her face as her jaw dropped. No sound was heard but I assumed a screamed left her lips and according to my memory, it had.

Damn. It was too late. I had lost her. From memory I knew she had a fear inside of her that would keep her from looking into the mirror again.

As a sense of my failure washed over me. My jaw dropped in frustration. I could no longer hold in my scream. I wanted to yell her name or do something drastic to get her to look at me, but I only had disappointment to bear.

Before I could make another move, the mirror faded, disappearing before my eyes. Ahead in the distance, another image appeared. The pinprick of light grew on me, calling to me, satisfying my need to be surrounded by something familiar. I wanted to escape the darkness and the only option I had was to pursue this light.

I approached, seeing the scene quite clearly. The dimly lit room adjacent to the studio with the large bed and silken sheets. The plush sofa sat across from the bed near the fake tree in the corner of the room. The tree had been placed to bring brightness to the space but only reminded me of all the things that didn't have life.

I watched as clean shaven and bright-eyed Nolan prepped a bottle of wine, popping the cork and pouring the red liquid into two wine glasses. While the other Rhea fussed around with the bedsheet, he added something extra to her glass. A crushed pill that quickly fizzled and dissolved in the dark liquid. Surprised by his behavior but not by the outcome, I gasped. I had suspected something other than wine was in that cup. My gut told me not to trust wholeheartedly, and I wonder if it was the ghostly Rhea, me, who acted as my intuition at the time.

Behind me, another scene came to fruition, calling me to witness the events as if a light had flickered on. I looked over my shoulder at the other Rhea lying naked on the bed, tangled in the satin sheets with an equally naked Nolan. He draped his body over hers. His milk-bronze skin grabbed my attention, but the thrusting of his hips stole it away. My eyes zeroed in on his muscular thighs as he sank into her. His lips glided across her neck and along her shoulder, never leaving her body. Her eyes remained closed, but she looked far from bliss. Was she present or in another world, a dark place?

As I replayed the memory of the scene in my mind, I remembered the pleasure Nolan delivered with his touch. But from this perspective, Rhea a peacefulness swept across her face as if she was dreaming, experiencing serenity in another land.

"What are you doing, Rhea?" I shook my head at the sight before me. How could I ignore so many red flags and still fall for Nolan's manipulation? I felt sorry for the girl I used to be. If only she had the strength to leave sooner.

The presence of another person within the vicinity startled me and I turned to see my body floating. It was her, the other Rhea, eyes closed, suspended in like a mermaid resting in invisible waters. Her eyes opened, landing on me and her jaw dropped before she disappeared.

How could she leave? Again, I had missed my chance to warn her, to tell her the truth about her beloved Nolan.

I searched the area, following a pull in my gut that assured me I would see her again. And like my gut had alerted, there she was. She stood far enough in the distance to be safe but close enough for me to see the panic in her eyes.

My jaw dropped, as she focused on me. This time, I needed to be careful not to scare her but alert her of what she was in for.

"You're broken." I made sure to be clear but gentle. "You don't want this. You have to leave."

She shook her head in confusion. Her eyebrows lowered and wrinkled her forehead in a way I never knew it could do. "What?" Her voice shook as she spoke.

Did she not understand? Could she not hear me? Or was she confused by what she saw? She had to leave the studio before Nolan could hurt her again, but this time I raised my voice to get the message across. "Now!" The sound of my unearthly growl rattled the fog around us, and she once again disappeared only to appear behind me.

The location was different, but she was closer, clearer, standing beside the bed with the satin sheet wrapped around her naked frame. Out of fear, she raised her shaky arm and pointed at... me.

Her eyes widened. "There. Look. Something's there. You see it?"

Time had forwarded in a split second, leaving me even more confused as I tried to figure out what was happening. She was talking about me, pointing to me, looking at me. So, she could see me! Excitement shot through me like adrenaline. Maybe now we could communicate. If I could get her to listen, maybe I could help her.

Nolan sat on the edge of the messy bed stained with sweat. His bright blue eyes landed on me, nearly connecting with mine, but became vacant when he shook his head. "I don't see anything."

"It's a dark ... thing. A shadow." She clenched the sheet near her bare chest. "Maybe it's her. That girl."

My eyes widened at the memory of this scene. Nolan and I were in bed, even then I was confused at seeing the ghost. I wasn't sure if I were dreaming or not, and Nolan tried to assure me that everything was peachy cobbler.

It wasn't.

He stood from the bed, not at all concerned about his nakedness. "Let me get you another drink. It'll relax you. Trust me." He headed toward the kitchen.

The wine. He was going to pour her another cup of that suspicious wine. I had to stop her from drinking any more of it, but I wasn't sure how. Was I able to interact with objects in the room? I had never tried, but I had to before Nolan convinced her to take another sip of that spiked drink.

I darted across the room, feeling the strands of my hair blow back from the speed. Nolan stopped in his tracks as if frightened by my swiftness. I was certain he could see me as his head darted in my direction as I zipped into the kitchen.

With a grunt, I pushed the bottle. But my palms didn't register the cold, smooth texture of the lass or its weight. It was as if my energy caused the bottle to topple over the edge of the counter and shatter on the floor.

Feeling depleted and exhausted from that one act, I bent and rested my hands on my knees. Watching as their eyes no longer targeted me but the broken glass.

"I—how did?" He stuttered. "The wine."

"I told you I saw something." She pointed near where I stood. "It's a woman that looks just like me. I think she's haunting us. Maybe she's haunting this room or the entire studio."

I shook my head, now understanding the truth of the situation.

"Rhea," Nolan finally turned to her, "take a deep breath. Calm down, alright?"

"But you saw it, didn't you? You saw the shadow."

"No. I didn't see a shadow or a woman," he lied. "What happened was the bottle fell off the counter. I must've placed it too close to the edge." He groaned and ran his hand through his hair. Even then, I spotted fear and confusion in his eyes. "Relax, Rhea. I'll clean it up. Cleaning up messes is my specialty."

As he bent to gather pieces of broken glass from the floor, his double with the bloody arms and sunken eyes stood in his place, watching me.

# 13

## CHAPTER 13

The ghostly Nolan floated inches above the ground. Missing buttons on his dingy white shirt brought my attention to it and the rolled-up sleeves. His frail arms no longer displayed the attractive muscle and definition I had become used to.

The way the toes of his dress shoes scraped the ground as he moved toward me prompted me to back away, unable to tear my eyes from the horrid site before me.

"Stay with me." His disembodied voice groaned from behind him as if demanding instead of pleading. "We'll be together forever."

"What are you doing here?" I shook my head, confusion and fear causing my lips to tremble.

"I'm here for you. Only for you. Don't leave me, Rhea."

I backed away, keeping a gap between us. The distant sound of a machine beeping took my attention, and my eyes followed the noise. A light far ahead highlighted the hospital room with injured Rhea in bed. Her head remained wrapped in loose gauze as she continued to be surrounded by the same posters and pictures of get well wishes and support.

The beeping chimed from the machine connected to her, measuring her vitals. I imagined the beeps matched her heartrate, steady and ongoing.

My eyes connected with his sunken, dark eyes again. "Stay away from me, Nolan," I shouted. Words that should have left my lips years ago.

I rushed toward the brightly lit room to get away, but the more I ran, the further it seemed. And with every step, ghostly Nolan followed.

"You can't go. I won't let you." He followed behind, hovering inches from the ground like a half-deflated balloon attached to me by an invisible thread. "You belong here with me, and I'll make sure you'll stay this time."

I picked up speed to put more space between him and myself, hoping to step foot inside the brightly lit hospital room ahead. Still, no matter how hard I ran, how fast my feet were, the room evaded me.

As the injured Rhea lay in the hospital bed, covered in a white sheet from the neck down, her exposed arms and face seemed to be more transparent than the last time. What was happening? Why could I see the pillow she lay on through her earlobe?

Before I could let my thoughts register, Nolan pounced on me from behind and I hit the floor with a thud. I managed to roll over as he straddled me, pinning me down with an immense weight. "Get off of me!" I pushed at his chest, trying to knock him away.

"You're not leaving me this time," he growled through clenched teeth, although his lips never moved. He managed to grab my wrists and pin them to the ground at my sides.

"Tell me what you want, and I'll give it to you." I pleaded with my eyes, hoping he would hear the pain and fear in my voice and take pity on me. "Just talk to me, Nolan. We can figure it out together. Okay?"

His sunken gaze locked onto me, sending a chill down my spine. He continued to keep me pinned under him but spoke. "Let her go and stay here with me." He looked up at the diminishing Rhea in the hospital bed. "She's almost gone. Let her go. Don't try to change it. Then I'll have you forever, like it's meant to be."

I nodded, agreeing. "Okay. I'm done. I don't want to fight anymore."

He sneered. His eyelids lowered in a glare. Did he know what I was up to? Did he suspect something by sensing my bullshit? "You said that before." His voice was low and full of bass. "You lie."

His boney fingers dug into my arm, keeping me anchored under him and on my back. "I don't want to fight, Nolan. I can't win. I know that now. Please." I begged with my eyes and held my breath as his grip slowly weakened. "I give up," I said, turning my head to the side, watching the light of the hospital room slowly fade with my words.

He loosened his grip and once again hovered above me. Watching, waiting, testing. I pushed myself up to my feet as he remained close in proximity. He inched so close if he had breath, I would have felt its moist heat on my skin.

The only thing I felt at the moment was a cold chill as my mind urged me to run and not look back. So, I did.

I turned toward the pinprick of light and ran as fast as my legs would carry me. The wind blew through my hair, and my arms pumped at my sides like an Olympian.

Somewhere in the surrounding space, Nolan's angry cries echoed. "Rhea, you bitch."

The anger in his voice lit a fire under me. The last time he called me a bitch was during an argument about the burger and fries I had eaten before a brand sponsored photoshoot. The same anger spewed from his voice now.

I didn't look back. I ran for what seemed like hours but was only minutes until a sight before me stopped me in my tracks. There he was, the ghastly Nolan who had been chasing me now stood several feet before me. His focus was no longer on me but the person in the center of the dimly lit room that manifested from the darkness.

It was the other Nolan in the familiar bedroom. He stood next to the bed and its strewn satin sheets, fully clothed, hair neatly styled on his head, and his phone in his palm. Whatever he was doing, like a magnet it attracted ghostly Nolan's attention.

I didn't mind that their attention was on his phone, I welcomed it because that meant it wasn't on me. Although, I too, grew curious. What were they looking at?

Without bringing attention to myself I focused on the phone in Nolan's hand. His text messages were open and the pretty face of the icon at the top of the text was Joselyn's. They were exchanging messages about her plans to meet with film execs in California and he agreed to send her money. And judging from the number of zeros in the amount, it was a large sum.

Had he been financially investing in her career, using the money we made from my sponsors? He never told me any of this. And seeing this now made me realize that he had been planning on keeping secrets all along. I knew he would try to find an excuse as to why he made these decisions without my knowledge. That's how he was. Never in the wrong.

A lump formed in my throat, and I gulped. Had he been sleeping with Joselyn too? I shook my head, trying to get the image out of my mind. Maybe it was my insecurities getting the best of me. Maybe he never went that far with her and never would. Could I trust that she was a good friend and would never allow such a thing even if he had offered.

There I was again, justifying his actions, trying not to make him seem like the bad guy, forgetting he was the reason I was in this place. And by the sound of ghostly Nolan's explanation, maybe there was a way to fix this. Maybe there was a way to get out of here.

Was my body hanging on to life in that hospital bed? Had my spirit somehow become trapped in this place? I'm sure Nolan's plan was to keep me here until my physical body died and I would be imprisoned here with him forever.

If I was a spirit, how did his ghostly equivalent get here? Was his body somehow in the same position as mine, hanging on to life while his ghost haunted me?

I didn't have much time to think about it, as ghostly Nolan began to move, pulling me from my thoughts and back to the event playing out before me.

His interest was fully on Nolan, circling him, watching him and his every move. Even though the handsome, healthy Nolan kept his focus on his phone and what he was doing, his ghostly counterpart was far too interested to even glance my way.

I took the opportunity to back away from the scene. When I left them far in the distance, I turned to find another pinprick of light.

Once locked on, I moved toward it, seeing the lively Rhea sitting at the small desk in the brightly lit and empty studio.

The click-clack of Joselyn's high heels as she disappeared around the corner to Nolan with his coffee on a tray rang in my ears. I watched as that Rhea took a sip of her iced coffee through the straw, her attention elsewhere but on the cryptic internet ad onscreen.

A repeat of the pest control advert played. Text on the screen said, "Run don't walk," referring to their services.

If only she could see it and take the warning. She needed to get out of there before it was too late. She needed to take the cue and leave the studio before Nolan could hurt her. I stepped to the computer, trying to tap the screen and get her attention.

Although my fingers attempted, they couldn't react with the laptop. Similar to the wine bottle, my fingers slipped through it as if nothing was there. Nervously, I tapped my fingers against my thigh, matching the sound of the ad as I absentmindedly tried to come up with another plan. That's when I realized my finger taps not only matched the rhythm of the annoying beeping sound from the ad, but also matched her tempo as she drummed her fingers on the desktop.

She finally looked up at the computer screen, reading the warning. Maybe I could use my habits to get through to her. Maybe there was a way. When her eyes widened at what wasn't just a coincidence, I sighed in relief.

The only thing I had to do now, was figure out a way to interact with her. If I could stop her from angering Nolan, maybe I could prevent the event that led me here. I just had to find a way.

Ghostly Nolan wouldn't be a problem if I had managed to escape him and if he was highly and easily distracted. All I had to do was figure out a way to communicate with that Rhea and urge her to leave before Nolan could lay his hands on her.

I looked ahead in my memory, remembering what would happen next. Joselyn would stay and help with another photoshoot, she would fetch us lunch, and after she leaves, Nolan and I would talk. During our talk he would mention needing to check emails and wanting to take a nap. I will leave him to return to my computer, where I confess everything to my audience.

I needed to prepare for that, but how?

The beeping of the hospital machinery chimed in the background. This time, the beeping that I assumed matched the beat of my heart, began to slow. Shit, what If I didn't have enough time? What if I took too long and the beeping stopped, would it be too late?

**14**

CHAPTER 14

The steady beep, beep, beep of the hospital machine harassed my ears. As every second ticked by, my anxiety increased knowing the beeping would continue to slow. If the machine slowed to a stop, flatlined, that would mean my body gave up. There was no turning back from that.

Standing in a shroud of blackness made me realize how alone I truly was. Not only was I alone now but had been for years. For so long, fans had been my only friends and family. Now Nolan and time threatened to trap me in this space without ever getting to say goodbye to Mom. I wondered how she was dealing with her only daughter holding onto life in a hospital bed. Did she know Nolan was the reason I wouldn't be able to make amends, speak to her, or ever again feel her embrace?

Mom didn't agree with my career, my love life, or many of my life choices, but suddenly I wish to hear it from her in person. Would I die without every telling her she had been right about Nolan, and I should've listened?

I couldn't stay in my thoughts for long. As much as I wanted to focus on Mom, my attention went to the spotlight ahead that highlighted me and Nolan in the dimly lit bedroom adjacent to the pristine photography studio.

I moved closer, taking in the scene.

There was no doubt Nolan was an attractive man. I was sure his sharp jawline was one of the reasons I couldn't resist him for so long. I watched as he removed his tailored dark blue blazer and tossed it on the edge of the bed. He fingered the cuff of his long-sleeved white button-down shirt. "What a day, yeah?" He sighed and gestured to the other Rhea who wore dark circles around her eyes like accessories. "Come, you sexy vixen." He crooked a finger and showcased his deep cheek dimples with a smile.

She moved toward his arms without question, like a magnet to iron. "We haven't had a chance to really talk about last night."

I thought back to what she was referring to. The wine bottle. She was talking about her witnessing me knock the bottle onto the floor.

"That's because there's nothing to talk about." His aroused, bedroom eyes looked more like Rhea's tired stare. I questioned if he had ever really been in the mood for sex at all or was only trying to smooth things over with her. "You had a good time, didn't you?"

"Honestly, it's all a bit of a blur." Her facial expression told of her confusion. "But that wine—"

"It was too close to the edge. Nothing else." His fingertips traced her jaw. "You're too sexy to worry about shattered wine bottles." His lips grazed hers, and although she didn't close her eyes like he did, she didn't acknowledge my presence. I was well hidden in the dark mist, glaring at his disgusting response.

When he broke the kiss and slid his palms down the sides of her body. She didn't seem to find comfort in his touch. I hadn't realized that my body language spoke volumes. Did he ignore the signs or truly didn't see it? If memory served me right, I had constantly been on edge during the time and sex was the last thing on my mind. She went on, "We never talked about what happened before the wine. You hurt me, Nolan."

I nodded, agreeing even though she couldn't see. That phone to the gut, his harsh and dismissive words... Yes, he hurt me, but that was nothing compared to what he would eventually do.

"Hurting you was a mistake I made up for by making you scream my name in pleasure."

I scoffed when she did. "Are you serious?"

"Rhea Patel ..." he rubbed his nose, annoyed.

"Nolan Hudson," she glared.

"We're better now," he said. "Why rewind time just to relive the pain? Let's move on, yeah?"

Move on is what I wished to do, but now in this state, I had no choice. I had to relive the pain, and I hoped the purpose was to somehow change it.

He lifted his phone. "I'm gonna respond to some emails and then climb into bed to get some shuteye before dinner. How does that sound?"

When that Rhea left him alone in the room, I expected the scene to fade away or the lights to go out and envelope me in darkness like before, but that didn't happen.

Instead, I watched as Nolan sat in the edge of the bed. I glanced around, waiting to see why the scene remained.

He lifted his phone and lowered it before even looking at it. Confused, I moved closer, trying to decipher what was happening and why he stared ahead at nothing.

When I turned to follow his line of sight, I saw what had grabbed his attention.

There, in the corner of the room, hovered the gaunt and ghastly version of Nolan. His limbs dangled at his sides, allowing the red liquid to glisten on his forearms. His head dipped to the side and forward, giving off dead and disturbed energy.

I nearly gasped at the sight but stifled it. My eyes widened at the realization that Nolan watched his dreary ghost, and his ghostly counterpart stared back.

Neither took notice of me. I was sure the hovering figure knew I was there but chose not to interact since finding a new interest. He floated toward Nolan and Nolan responded by laying back on his elbows on the mattress to put space between them.

"I'm tired." Nolan closed his eyes and sat forward before rubbing his temples. "I must've caught whatever bug Rhea has."

The bloodied apparition shook his head, getting Nolan's attention again. He didn't even move his mouth to talk as if he knew talking was pointless and Nolan wouldn't be able to hear him. He pointed a bony finger, aiming at the phone in Nolan's grip.

Nolan frowned but glanced at the phone.

Curiously, I focused on what was onscreen. A notification of Rhea going live on UpTube lit up his screen on cue.

"Huh? What is this? What the hell is she doing?" Nolan shook his head but clicked on the banner. It took him to the live stream of the other Rhea talking to our community of followers. I took note of his username, and realized it was a totally different user and account.

Had he always been following me from different secretive accounts?

I didn't move or make a peep as I wanted to stay in the shadows and out of sight as possible. But watching his reaction, the distain and anger bubbling to the surface to twist his face in disgust worried me.

I knew exactly what would happen next. He would confront Rhea and it will lead the most gruesome fight we ever had. But what I didn't expect was to see Nolan's facial features match his ghostly counterpart.  The look in the ghastly figure's hollow eyes sent an icy chill down my spine, especially when he motioned to Nolan by swiping his thumb across his neck from one ear to the other.

I gasped and looked around for the other Rhea. This was my chance to warn her. I had to persuade her to leave the building as soon as possible. But I didn't know where to start or how to find her. I turned to run through the darkness, searching for another pinprick of light but only pitch black surrounded me.

Frustrated I called out. "Rhea? You need to run. Run, Rhea. If you can hear me, run!" But still, nothing happened or changed.

My hearted pounded, but the distant, faint sound of familiar beeps slowed. It didn't match my heartbeat at all, it matched hers. The Rhea still in the present reality, who was still fighting for her life.

I had to do something. I ran as fast as my legs would carry and only stopped several minutes later when my legs refused to go on. Feeling defeated, I collapsed to the ground. This time, the cold of the tile floor chilled my skin. Were the tiles from the studio floor?

With that thought, the light switched on, blinding me even though I put my hand up to shield it. The surreal environment felt more like a dream than reality, but the cold and solitude hit me like a truck anchoring me in the truth.

The sound of my voice perked my ears, and the sound became clearer along with my vision. The voice came from her, the other Rhea sitting at the small desk in the corner of the large white room. The flash mount umbrellas were still in position before the backdrop feet from the desk. A few empty clothes racks stood in the middle of the room.

I got up to move closer to the desk. The open laptop was the only thing between me and Rhea. Her eyes landed on me, but she continued to speak to her audience through the camera. "I've been so stressed lately that I swear I'm seeing things that would make me seem crazy if I didn't think others didn't see them too."

She had been more on target than she knew with that statement. She wasn't the only one seeing things, unfortunately Nolan would never admit that.

Her eyes scanned my dark teal SSL athletic leggings and matching tank top. I realized the only thing that differentiated us was our hairstyles, her sloppy ponytail kept the strands from obstructing her face. My hair framed my head with floating red locks, not doing much to disguise the numb gaping wound at the side of my head.

Her eyes on me, she continued to speak to her followers. "I don't know what I should do, but I know I need things to change."

Anticipation caused my fingers to tap, tap, tap my thigh as my mind raced with possibilities. Then I caught her fingertips as they rhythmically tapped the desk. They mimicked mine, stopping when mine did.

We tilted our heads at the same time in confusion, and we refused to take our eyes from one another.

"I'll talk to you all about it more later. For now, I have to let you go." She ended the stream and our eyes stayed glued. "Who are you?"

I had her undivided attention and this time she didn't seem frightened of me. This was my chance. I took my cue from the ghostly Nolan and used body language to convey my message. I was more than sure speaking would be to no avail.

The popular pest control ad repeated on the bottom banner of her computer screen, but she was too focused on me to see it. My eyes widened as I lifted an arm to point to the computer. "You need to get out of here," I said, even if she couldn't hear me.

She pressed her forefinger to her chest, trying to guess what I was communicating but she missed the mark. Then her gaze dropped to the computer screen before her. The same ad continued to play. Although the sound had been muted, the words "Run don't walk" stood out.

I saw the moment her heart sank. She turned paler than the room's walls and her arms dropped to her sides.

"Are you trying to tell me something?" Her chest rose and fell rapidly, fear registered in her big brown eyes. "Is this a warning?"

My jaw dropped and I pointed to the sight behind her, but it was already too late.

"What is going on with you?" Nolan's words came out in a hushed growl. Directly over his shoulder hovered his dingy, emaciated, and silent ghost. "First, you wreck both of our careers on UpTube Live, and now you're talking to a wall?"

I let out a discouraged scream, but the lights went out leaving me in utter darkness.

# 15

## CHAPTER 15

The lights came back on, but instead of the brightly lit white room of the photography studio, the light brightened the hospital room and bed where my body lay. Fresh vases of bright flowers accompanied the posters and pictures made by my fans.

Even the potent smell of roses filled my nostrils and flushed out any trace of the astringent sterile smell of the hospital.

I stood, tempted to walk toward my body, with tubes hooked up to it leading to machines and monitors, but as I stepped toward the scene, the entire room glided back as if on a conveyer belt. No matter how fast or slow I walked or ran, the entire room shifted, keeping one step out of my reach.

My body lay motionless on the hospital bed except for the steady rise and fall of the abdomen with each breath. The more I looked at it, the more I realized how translucent it had become. How much time had passed? How long has my body been lying there?

With the thought of being alone in the room, the door to the room opened. Beyond the open entry was still, quiet and the same blackness that constantly enveloped me. It was only when Joselyn walked through that I could make her out, appearing like a beautiful bridesmaid carrying a bouquet of red roses through the fog.

My heart skipped a beat in excitement, and I could have sworn the machine connected to my body spiked in rhythm, too.

"Jos?" I called out, but of course she didn't acknowledge me.

She shambled to the edge of the bed to sit. She didn't seem to notice how the wrinkled white sheets beneath were visible through the limbs of my body. With her head down, tears glistened on her cheek, and she stared at the monitor and the lines and numbers that scrolled across the screen. "Why, Rhea? Why you? Why now? You had such a wonderful future ahead. I can't believe that was taken from you."

I nodded, agreeing with her when she muttered, "He belongs in jail for what he did." She caressed a rose petal with her fingers, nearly plucking it off absentmindedly. "I know you probably can't hear me, but I want you to know that your fans miss you. Hell, I miss you. I'm sure Nolan misses you, too."

"No. Nolan can rot in hell." I sneered at her comment. Didn't she know? Hasn't what he's done made headlines by now? I searched my mind for an explanation, but couldn't come up with anything to explain why she would say such a thing.

"I hope they find the guy who hit you and shove his car up his ass for leaving the scene." She wiped the flowing tears from her rosy, red cheeks with her bare palm like a toddler. "This world is so fucked. But don't worry, I'm sure Nolan's looking down at you, giving you the strength to pull through and fully recover."

"Looking down on me? Are you kidding?" I couldn't stop my head from shaking in confusion and disappointment, even as she pulled a torn sliver of paper from her pocket and unfolded it. "So, Nolan is really dead?" I asked her, knowing she wouldn't respond but couldn't help speaking it aloud. "He died? How?" I had hoped she would've known the truth, or at least suspected it, but she seemed oblivious to the entire situation.

Distracted by the words on the piece of paper, she silently read over it, folded it back up, and stuffed it back in her rear pocket. Once secured in her pocket, her face twisted in emotional discomfort again, and she hurled herself over my body and sobbed uncontrollably.

Her abrupt actions took me aback, but I shook away my reservations. "Where is Nolan, Jos?" I asked again, hoping she would somehow hear me and answer. Was his body lying in a hospital bed, too? Was he barely hanging on like I was, or was he finished? "Is he dead? Jos, answer me?"

"I'm here." The bass in Nolan's voice rattled inches from my ear. Startled, I turned, leaving the false safety of the hospital room and Jos to fade to the blackness behind me. "I missed you, baby. I'm not going anywhere." His toes pointed toward the ground as he hovered. His sunken face emphasized his deep cheek dimples and chiseled jawline, making him appear like a typical movie villain and nothing like the healthy, athletically fit man I fell in love with.

"Are you dead? Did you die?" I backed away, but he drifted toward me, keeping pace with my steps.

He lifted his arms, showcasing the crimson wounds and the stains they left on his forearms. "I did it for you."

I brought my hand to my mouth to suppress my scream. "Why?" I spoke through my fingers, afraid to remove my hand and reveal my revolt.

"To be with you." His eyes held no personality, no charm like they used to. A void, only emptiness, stared back at me. "I've meant it when I said I'd die without you. I'd stop at nothing to keep you. You're mine."

"Oh, my god!" The realization of what was happening hit me and I turned to run. Again, not knowing where I was heading, but my aim was to put as much space between me and him as possible.

I didn't feel the impact of the ground beneath my feet, but I ran regardless, making headway, refusing to look behind me. Afraid that he would be on my heels and slow me if I dare attempted to glance.

But what caught my attention up ahead halted me on the spot.

Nolan, in all his naked glory, sprawled on the sofa of his apartment. A few years younger, possessing the handsome looks of any rock star or athlete I ever witnessed without the need to possess the talent. Perfect hair slicked back on his head, beautifully kept eyebrows that framed his robust face, yet completely hairless on every other part of his body. In the low light of the fireplace, he showcased the muscles and definition that would make anyone swoon.

In fact, I remembered him being in that exact position. It was after signing my first huge fashion deal. We were celebrating the achievement as it marked the first huge milestone in my career. The bottles of liquor sat on the coffee table arranged out of the way of the warm, crackling fire.

There I was, approaching him with a strawberry in one hand and a can of whipped cream in the other as he lay enticingly on the sofa. My bare breasts caught his attention first and then his eyes travelled to the pair of black lace panties that made up my entire ensemble. The yellow and orange light of the dancing flame flickered on her tanned skin.

From directly behind me in the darkness, Nolan's haunting voice whispered, "We were perfect, weren't we?"

I refused to turn and acknowledge him or to even run to get away. What was the point? But a chill crept down my spine, reminding me that in this space I wasn't alone. I kept my eyes glued to my past self as she straddled the man on the sofa. "You deserved better, Rhea." I shook my head, feeling the heaviness of sadness in my chest. Of course, that version of me didn't know what was destined for her in this relationship. She didn't know the pain, control, and lack of freedom she would encounter with the tantalizing man of her dreams.

The ghastly presence of Nolan remained at my back. "This was the first time we professed our love. Do you remember?" His voice sent an icy unease along the hairs at the back of my neck, but I still refused to turn or answer him.

In fact, I didn't want to see him at all. Just the thought of him floating inches above the ground with the lack of personality I grew accustomed to was bad enough. But the gruesome wounds on his arms, the blood, and the distant look on his face, void of any pleasantness, triggered my fight-or-flight response. The fact that he was the reason I was now in this dark and eerie realm—

A squeal of laughter brought my attention to the bliss on her face. The fun and pleasure she experienced, and then Nolan said it, "I love you." The man who had wrapped that Rhea in his arms whispered it in her ear just as the ghastly creature behind me whispered it I mine. "I love you, Rhea. You're mine forever."

Rhea tossed her head back in glee, red hair flung behind her as she moaned in pleasure, smiled in bliss, and rode the handsome beast. "I love you, forever."

An icy hand on my arm spun me around, forcing me to investigate the pale and sunken face of the man I used to know. "See? We belong together," he declared without moving his mouth.

I didn't have to look behind me to know the scene had dissipated. The light, warmth, and energy of that memory were long gone. Faded and possibly never to return.

"What's the point of this?" I finally asked, searching the two hollow holes on his face for some resemblance of a man. "Why am I here?"

"To surrender." He emphasized the S in the word, making it slither from his lips like a serpent, although his mouth remained closed. His icy palm crept up my arm, but no matter how much he tried to calm me, it did the opposite. "Submit."

"No." I pulled my arm from his grip.

His brow bone accentuated as he glared. "You're ill, Rhea." He shook his head, and as he did, the familiar handsome man looked back at me. "You're ill and now I must figure out what to do about that."

"What?" Confused, I backed away and only when my vision read-justed that I recognized the brightly lit studio and the other Rhea in the place I had just been standing.

"You're utterly insane to say what you said on a public platform," he continued, speaking to her. They both looked distressed and like they hadn't met sleep for some time. "I saw it all. Apparently, you never wanted to be the spokesperson for SSL? Well, that's news to me, especially since you signed the contract, Ms. Rhea Patel."

I moved to investigate the look on her face. "No, I didn't like how they implied only certain types of people could wear their clothes." Her voice raised as if she were finally releasing her unbridled frus-trations. "I told you that, and you, yes you, Mr. Nolan Hudson, convinced me to sign the contract because it was 'a great financial move.' So, thank you for convincing me to sell my soul."

Oh no. I recognized this moment. I knew exactly what was happening and what would happen next. Panic rushed through me, causing me to freeze.

He chuckled. "So, now I forced your signature on that contract?"

"I had morals." She sneered at him in disgust, and I sensed the frustration in her voice.

This was it. This was the moment I dreaded, but all I could do was watch.

"What is morality when there's money involved?" He scoffed and stuffed his hands in his pant pockets.

Rhea shook her head, and from this perspective I could see in her face that she was finally done with his shit. Could he sense it, too? She went on, "You don't care about me. This whole relationship is based on padding your pockets. Just admit it."

"How dare you say that!" He placed his hand over the empty space in his chest where his heart should have been. "It's clear you have no idea how much I love you. Sure, the money is great, but I will literally lay down and die for you. After all these years, how can you not see it?"

They continued arguing, but from behind handsome Nolan appeared the gruesome ghoul who resembled him. The haunting figure leaned toward Nolan to press his lips to Nolan's ear and whispered things I could only imagine.

My body wouldn't move, my mouth wouldn't speak. I could only stare and watch, fully aware and not prepared for what was coming next.

**16**

## CHAPTER 16

"It's clear you have no idea how much I love you. Sure, the money is great, but I will literally lay down and die for you. After all these years, how can you not see it?" As Nolan spoke to the other Rhea, his ghastly double remained at his side, murmuring into his ear.

What did he whisper? I sneered at the thought, the possibilities. Even as I contemplated, a dark angry energy formed around them both as a dense black mist. It contrasted the stark white that surrounded us all in the studio.

Of course, the other Rhea didn't see it and therefore didn't react to it. She only shook her head at his words. "You say that every time I threaten to leave and live my life the way I want. That's always been your way of making me feel guilty, so I stay, and we make love, and the cycle continues. But not anymore, Nolan. It ends today."

I nodded. "Yes," I whispered. Maybe like ghost Nolan, my words could somehow make it into her ears and penetrate her mind. "The cycle ends today."

Nolan gulped and sighed. "Rhea, come on now. Listen—"

I shook my head at his attempt to change her mind. She answered, "No, I'm always listening. That's all I do, but when is it my turn to start being listened to? If you really loved me or cared, you would've told me you wanted to manage Joselyn Murphy's acting career. But you didn't because that's a conflict of interest and you know I wouldn't have agreed."

"So, she told you, huh?" He dropped his gaze, but my eyes went to his bloody look-a-like hovering at his shoulder. The bridge bone of his eyebrows became more prominent, showcasing his scowl.

As the couple continued arguing I glanced behind them at the door that led to the hall and the adjacent apartment.

With the mere thought of the apartment, the environment changed, and I found myself in the kitchen next to the bar counter. I glanced around the space, taking it in. The low lights set the warm tone and for a second I wondered how I had made the transition and what it signified.

I couldn't think long as the traces of sweet wine entered my nostrils, briefly distracting me. I glanced at the floor where cherry red stained the grout of the tiles, reminding me of two things; the shattered bottle of the tampered liquor, and the liquid that pooled around my head as I had lay on that very floor.

My gaze snapped to the hefty diamond shaped trophy on the counter with my name and the words "top multiracial fashion influencer" etched on the glass. An idea popped into my mind. If Nolan couldn't see the trophy, he wouldn't use it to hurt her.

From the other room, my voice reverberated through the space before reaching my ears. "I'm calling my mom and telling her I'm finally coming home, because I'm not staying here one more night."

"Are you serious?" Nolan's voice grew aggressive as it trailed my voice from somewhere outside of my immediate space. "You'd reconcile with that woman after the things she's said about you, us, and your career? She wished ill on you for choosing the path you chose."

"I'm sure she'd be forgiving knowing I'm choosing a different one now." There was a short pause before my familiar voice continued. "Give me my phone, Nolan."

"I can't let you make that mistake. You'll thank me later. Trust me."

I remembered. Nolan had taken my phone and placed it in his pants pocket. And if my memory were right, he and she would enter this room at any second. I kept my eyes on my goal, readying my hands to push the trophy from the counter before they made it to the room.

Inches from the heavy glass on its shallow pedestal, I pushed my hands toward the trophy. It wobbled on its stand before my hands went through it completely. I gasped at the progress and prepared myself to try again. Never one to give up on the first, second, or third try. To my surprise, instead of the other Rhea and Nolan entering the space, bloody Nolan interrupted my process instead.

"You're wasting your time." His voice startled me, and I froze, staring into the two dark holes in his head where his steel blue eyes should have been. "The outcome is inevitable, baby. Don't try to fight it."

Before I could respond, the couple entered the space.

"I can't believe you're doing this," the other Rhea told Nolan who followed behind her.

In a nonchalant manner, he said, "You know I know what's best for you. Have I steered you wrong yet?"

"So ridiculous," I murmured, amazed that her lips matched my words as if she whispered them at the same time. She rushed around the room searching for her shoes while Nolan stood near the counter in the same spot his ghost hovered. He and his likeness crossed their arms, synchronizing their movements and unnervingly merged into one. The handsome, vibrant parts of him quickly faded into the gloomy, malicious man he had always hid away.

"Where are you going?" He sneered at her. "You're seriously not leaving. It's late and dark out there, Rhea. You can't go anywhere by yourself. Crazed fans exist, you know?"

She mimicked him and crossed her arms. "So, what are you gonna do? Hold me hostage?"

"I intend to protect you," he said matter-of-factly. "That's my job. That's what you hired me to do."

She paused, her eyes intent, sure, and unwavering. "I hired you as a manager to manage my career and I trusted you as a boyfriend to love me like I deserve, and now because you failed at both, you're fired." When those words left her mouth, I felt her power surged through me, and it felt good to hear her say what I'd been feeling for so long. I stared at Nolan just as she did and her and I both declared, "You, Mr. Nolan Hudson, are fired from ever again being associated with Rhea Patel or her likeness."

He pinched the bridge of his nose and sniffed, but what caught me off guard was the other Nolan who stepped forward. His eyebrow bridge had become even more prominent to form the beginnings of what looked like horns, making his facial features as deep-set and dark as any evil villain.

I gasped and backed up. "Stay away."

"Never." He continued to move forward, prompting me further from the trophy. "You." He bared his teeth like a wild and rabid beast. His even pearly whites where no more as what emerged from his receding gum-line were rows of sharp and rotten bone. "You've been a naughty bitch," he growled.

Before I got too far, I rushed toward the trophy. Like the wine bottle before, I pushed it, but instead of toppling to the ground it wobbled violently instead.

Everyone in the space paused and watched the award teeter back and forth on the edge of its base. The silence was so loud I could hear the soft plink-plunk sound of the glass. Momentum finally urged it over, and when it came crashing down, everyone jumped back with a collective gasp.

The trophy didn't shatter into a million pieces like I had expected, but rather, the glass simply remained intact.

"What?" I said aloud, but only ghastly Nolan seemed to hear me.

Did this mean I had changed the cycle? Would this lead to a new outcome?

Before I did anything else, ghostly Nolan turned to his handsome self. "End this," he demanded. Nolan's bright blue eyes widened, and that's when I knew he had recognized his demon.

While they were distracted, I turned to Rhea. "Run!" I screamed.

She shook her head at the splintered trophy. "I'm done with this." As she turned to leave, Nolan grabbed her ponytail, stopping her in her tracks.

"You're not going anywhere," he snarled.

Her and I both yelped. She reached behind her to pry his hands from her hair to no avail. "What are you doing? Stop, Nolan. Let me go."

"I can't do that." His eyes were on his ghost as he tugged her hair, causing her to fall back onto her ass. Her hair brushed her shoulders as it fell from the ponytail. A chunk of long red strands hung from the elastic band in his fist.

An icy shock hit my system from being forced to experience the tragedy unfold again. Even though I viewed it from a different perspective, it affected me just as much as the first time. Even her pain and fear overtook me.

But what was most interesting is the shock on her face when she looked at me. Her brown eyes glistened with tears as they locked onto mine.

Nolan's ghost got Nolan's attention by pointing to the trophy lying on the floor and with one fluid motion, the dark ghost mimed his request by sliding his thumb across his neck from one ear to the other. But most frightening was that handsome Nolan obeyed.

I pointed to the apartment door and instructed Rhea to, "Go, Rhea! Get out of here."

She managed to get to her feet, but Nolan had lifted the trophy in one hand like a baseball he readied to pitch.

I put my hands up to stop him. "No!" But he looked straight through me.

She turned just as the diamond shaped glass left his hand to impact her temple before clanking to the ground.

I grabbed my head from the pain as I watched her go down like a feather. But instead of lying there and staring up at the man that had called her his everything, she crawled on her belly toward the bloodstained award on the ground ahead of her.

Bright red blood gushed from the wound on her temple, and I pressed my palm against the painful indentation on mine, feeling the cold liquid pour over my fingers.

"Oh, fuck," Nolan whispered through trembling lips. "What have I done? Rhea, baby?"

His dark, eerie ghost followed her as she crawled across the floor. The look on his face was one of satisfaction as he hovered over her, waiting for her to take her last breath.

The excruciating pain brought me to my knees. And at the same time, she stopped crawling and collapsed to the floor. But none of us could take our eyes from her, as if expecting something extraordinary to happen next.

Just as her breathing stilled her, another phantom figure that resembled me squirmed beneath her. I wasn't the only to see it, ghastly Nolan saw it too.

"Come back to me," he hissed, encouraging the phantom to emerge. "Yes, come to me."

Confused, I looked down at the blood on my palm only to realize I could see straight through my hand. I was fading, and the other Rhea was too as the body lay on the tile floor in a growing puddle of red.

From the distance ... a sound.

"Eyes wide open."

"Stop!" I cried and Nolan's dark figure turned to me. "This stops now!" I howled, shaking the foundation I kneeled on.

Just then, the other Rhea lifted her head from the red puddle beneath her.

**17**

— ◆ —

## CHAPTER 17

The ghostly redhead had faded as the other Rhea lifted herself from the floor to crawl. I watched in awe as she fought to slither along the white tiled floor toward the apartment door. Would she make it beyond the threshold, to the photo studio, and out the front door of the building like I imagined was her goal?

Nolan's attention remained on his ghost as the dark figure hovered near the bar counter. His deep voice instructed Nolan to, "Get rid of her phone," and relied on a bad attempt of sign language to get his point across. Deep-set hollow eyes receded in his head. The look of utter anger exuded from the entity. "As long as you do what I say, you'll be fine."

It was amazing that the sight of him didn't scare Nolan. I imagined he had grown well acquainted with the figure as it represented all that he truly was but kept hidden from the world. It didn't surprise me at all that the most handsome and successful can hold onto such ugliness on the interior.

So many girls looked at Nolan as the perfect man, companion, and lover, but like me they were looking at him from inside a neat little bubble. Nolan had ejected me from that bubble quite harshly me from that bubble, and soon our fans, family and world would see

I too had an ugliness that consumed me. The fragile, naïve, girl afraid to use her voice or speak out when needed. And look where that led me. But now I was determined to make sure that version of me spoke up today.

While the two Nolans tried to communicate with each other, I went to Rhea's side. "Come on," I encouraged. "You need to get out of here." Her attention was on the blood pouring from her head and down the side of her face. I wasn't even sure she knew I was there, but I instructed her anyway. "Move faster, Rhea. You have to get out of here."

As I reached out to help pull her along, the transparency of my hand revealed the bright red pool of blood on the floor beneath her. Why was I fading? From what I had put together, I thought I would remain in the misty realm only if my physical body died. So why was I disappearing if Rhea and my physical body was still alive. Whatever was happening it was clear that I didn't have much time to figure it out.

Rhea collapsed again as her hands slipped on the growing puddle beneath her. It was then that I saw the phantom within her struggling to push itself up as well. It resembled me in every way, including the weightless strands of hair surrounding her injured head. If Rhea dies, will the phantom within her replace us both? Would that begin a new cycle, the final cycle as Nolan suggested?

"Get up." I tried to nudge the collapsed body but like every time before, my hands went straight through. Neither Rhea or her phantom acknowledged me or my efforts. In fact, it was as if I was invisible to everyone in the room.

Getting as close as I could, nearly mimicking her on the floor, a wave of relief briefly washed over me to see the subtle movement of her torso rise and fall with her breaths. She slowly blinked her eyes as if each time would be her last. Was she on the verge of giving up? Knowing myself, I was convinced she would just lie down and let her life drain. She had to know she still had a chance, and she had my support. I still existed for a reason, and that reason was to get her out of this hell.

I needed to do something to get her attention. I looked around for anything that could help. And while the Nolans continued to struggle with their communication and remain distracted, I worked on the splintered yet intact trophy.

If I can bring attention to it, maybe Rhea would see that she still had some fight left in her.

Again, I tried moving the heavy glass with my fingertips. I concentrated on the texture of it, imagining how it should feel on my fingers and how much effort it should take to slide it along the tiles. I concentrated so hard, my wounded temple throbbed and radiated heat.

"Come on," I whispered, mostly to myself. But Rhea's eyes snapped open and stayed fixed on nothing in particular. "Yes, yes. Come on." My eyes shifted from Rhea, to the Nolans, then back to the cracked diamond shaped glass.

The abrupt cold, smooth surface registered on my fingertips, and I grew excited. In the distance, the sound of my elevated heartbeat could be heard through the matching beeps of the hospital monitor. I didn't let it sidetrack me in my goal, but the distant beeping and my attempts seemed to grab the dark, grim figure's notice.

"Stop her!" His deep haunting voice shook the very space around us, but only I was thrown off balance.

His wafer-thin figure rushed toward me, but I managed to push the trophy before he tackled me and pinned me down.

"Run, Rhea!" I called out from beneath the ghoulish figure. I wasn't sure if she heard me or not, but she pushed herself up from the floor to get on her knees. Her sights on the trophy a few feet ahead.

Although handsome Nolan was nothing but when he quickly pulled the phone he took from her from his pocket and tucked it under the mattress of the bed. I screamed, watching him hide her quickest way to call for help and panicked at the reasons why he would want to.

I wrestled with his dark twin, trying desperately to free myself from his powerful grip. His angry scowl looked more like disappointment, especially when he cried, "Why are you making this difficult?"

I shook my head, not wanting to stare into his hollow eye sockets for too long. "I'm not gonna let her lie down and die for you."

"It's already done, Rhea. Stop trying to fight it." He turned to look at Nolan as he stood near the edge of the bed, frozen as he watched Rhea struggle to make it passed the open door.

"What have I done?" The fear and uncertainty in his shaky voice angered his dark companion. "Stop her!" he growled. "End this, you coward."

Startled, Nolan rushed forward toward the slowly crawling woman he claimed to love and respect for so many years. "I have to do this. For us," were his last words before rushing to her side and slipping on the trail of blood he tried to hop over.

As he went back, the thud of his head hitting the floor tiles rattled in my chest. "Rhea, run!" I called.

Ghastly Nolan squeezed my wrist so tight I was sure he would snap them from my phantom body. I screamed in pain, as his face came inches from mine. "You're ruining this. Stop trying to save her. It's pointless." He forehead came down on mine like a hammer, sending a sharp pain through my temple. I lay on the ground, surrounded by dark fog, with no intention of fighting to get up through the pain.

I only imagined Rhea felt the same.

Eerie Nolan hovered over his handsome likeness as he cradled his head groaned in pain. "You're a bloody failure. You don't deserve her for how you perform. Look at you, worthless." His face contorted into a mixture of evil, anger and disappointment. "All you had to do was what I told you. How can you be such a failure. You're not focused. What are you doing?"

Nolan squirmed on his back in the blood and reached inside his pant pocket to retrieve his cell phone. Instead of calling anyone, he ran his thumbs along the text pad.

While his ghost continued berating his physical self, I lay silently and watched as Rhea pushed herself from the bloody puddle to stand. I didn't make a sound as she bent to gather the trophy in her arms.

"You want to lose her?" Ghost Nolan went on, even kneeling to get closer and demand attention from his likeness. His focus solely on his pathetic physical self. "Have I steered you wrong, you bloody loser. Get up. Get up now and finish this."

I held my breath in anticipating as Rhea, stained in her own bright red blood from head to toe, shuffled toward Nolan and lifted the trophy.

"W-wait." He looked up at her and put his hand up. "Rhea, baby?"

His dark ghost stood and pivoted in the most unnatural choreography. "No!"

And down came the hefty, beautiful diamond shaped trophy. Somehow it managed to bounce off Nolan's head and onto the floor next to him. The impact instantly took him out and judging by the amount of blood spewing from his thick hair and trickling from his ears, he wouldn't be waking up.

With his ghost gone, I sat up, wondering what this meant. I was still here, the Nolan were gone, but something didn't feel right.

Rhea dropped to the floor next to Nolan's body and the trophy. The amount of blood over the tiles and splatters along the walls and furniture turned this once cozy apartment into the sight of a massacre.

Confused, I stood to get a closer look. She couldn't just collapse and die? And why would Nolan's ghost disappear upon Nolan's death? It wasn't until Rhea groaned in pain that a wave of relief washed over me. She was weak and losing blood but was still alive.

It wasn't until she reached for the trophy and let out a painful growl, that I realized why she sounded so defeated. The trophy had finally split in two and red tainting both pieces. But it was what was beneath the phone that made me realize this nightmare was nowhere near over. The trophy had somehow landed on the cell phone, her direct link to help, crushing it.

**18**

— ◆ —

## CHAPTER 18

I shook my head at the trophy as its two broken halves lay atop of the cell phone, all items covered in various sized droplets of splattered blood. The existing pool of crimson liquid melded with the blood that trickled from the top of Nolan's head. His thick, dark hair hid the resemblance between his cracked skull and the split trophy.

Rhea lay motionless in the puddle, her breathing slow and steady. The entire space looked more like a scene out of a massacre than a studio or apartment. The white tiled floors contrasted the deep red that spattered and gathered across it.

Out of nowhere, the dim light of the space quickly faded, leaving me in utter darkness. "Wait, no. I don't wanna leave. Not now." I turned, examining my surroundings, trying to get my bearings although I had no control. "I need to stay with her. She needs my help." Of course, my wishes went unanswered as the misty fog rushed in to cloak me in blackness.

Frustrated, confused, and exhausted, I walked in what felt like circles, going everywhere but getting nowhere. It wasn't until I stopped moving that a distant voice slowly became distinct.

The sounds of a young child speaking and laughing pulled me in, and before I knew it, I found myself approaching the ghost of Nolan from behind while he watched a wholesome scene play out before us. As a silent witness, I stopped and tried to put together the scene in front of me.

A little boy sat alone on the rug in a cozy room. He wrapped a baby doll in his arms, rocking it back and forth as he recited, "I'll protect you from all the bad people, especially momma and dadda. You'll be my friend forever."

The bright brown hair on the little boy's head matched the hair on the doll, and they both reminded me of Nolan. Were we enamored by a scene from his childhood?

The door to the room opened with a steady creak that only an old wooden door would make and immediately the little boy hid the doll behind his back. Even from this angle, it was obvious the doll wasn't well hidden.

"Who gave you that?" A mature female voice growled. "Winston," she called from over her shoulder. "You better come get a look at this?"

The name Winston Hudson belonged to Nolan's father. And even though every fiber in my being told me to find the other Rhea and help her get medical attention before our efforts were lost, curiosity compelled me to stay and watch. I needed to know what would happen and what it will lead to. There had to be a reason why I was a witness to this moment.

Winston approached the doorway, heavy boots clunk, clunk on the tired wooden floor with every step. I had never met him personally, but even the sounds of his footsteps were as menacing as Nolan described. He appeared in the doorway like a towering giant compared to everything else in the room. "Get rid of that damn doll, Nolan. That toy is a sign of weakness and no boy of mine will be seen as weak."

The lights shut off, casting me and ghost Nolan in darkness again. Like a flash, they immediately came back on to highlight a worn wooden dinner table in a cozy dining room. Three empty plates sat on round wicker place mats atop the table with carved notches and grimy scratch marks in its wood.

Still, Nolan stood before me, taking in the sights. He hadn't moved or turned to look over his shoulder since the scenes manifested before our eyes. I focused on the back of his head and knew he was either too enthralled or didn't care much to turn around and look at me.

Still, he stared at the scene as if he were compelled to. Even from my perspective, his face resembled him at his finest; clean shaven, neatly groomed, lightly sun kissed skin. Gone were the bloody forearms, the protruding eyebrow bone, and the sunken empty eye sockets.

The dinner table quickly filled up with food of all kinds, as if time sped up before our eyes. In the dining chairs appeared Winston with less of a hairline than in the scene before, his mother Clair who kept her fingers pressed to her temple, and a young Nolan in what looked like his teen years.

Nolan's facial hair hadn't grown in yet, and although his clothes were neat and clean, his long hair sat on his shoulders greasy and unkempt. He rolled a sweet pee on his plate, pushing it away with his fork only for it to roll back into the center of the dish. His ghostly version laughed while observing, just as he did at the dinner table, amused with playing with his food.

I kept silent, not wanting to bring attention to myself, but waiting to see if I'd learn anything new that could help me help Rhea.

His mother rubbed her temple in annoyance. "I've the bloodiest migraine all morning. Please, Nolan, be quiet."

"You heard your mother," Winston casually pointed his butter knife toward Nolan from across the table as he spoke. "Quiet at the dinner table. That means no snickering under your breath either."

The lights went out again, and I anticipated seeing him as an adult, but when the lights came back on the scene had changed to our first meeting at the coffee shop. Again, the lights flickered off and came back on to illuminate he and I making love on the kitchen counter after baking his favorite birthday cake, red velvet. I remember the evening being full of laughter as I continually teased him for refusing to confirm his age. The lights went out and shined again on the scene of us celebrating my first huge online sponsorship. The smiles on our faces were everything, too bad they would no longer light up any rooms.

The light went on and off again like a strobe light, highlighting different parts of our life together. It lit up all the laughter, bliss, and celebrations we shared. It quickly showcased all the good times that had kept me from leaving him earlier, holding on in the hopes of rekindling those special moments. As the lights continued to flicker on and off, Nolan grew uninterested and turned to face me instead.

The quick moving succession of our happy times continued like a projection on a screen, and as the lights flickered, Nolan slowly approached. I back up to keep distance between us, but as soon as the lights came back on, he was closer.

"What do you want?" I called out.

"You remember these moments?" Suddenly he was behind me, arms snaking around my waist. "This was us, happy, content, in love. Remember?"

Familiarity hit me when his strong arms embraced my body, still I pushed them away but he remained close. "I'm not scared of you."

"I don't want you to be." His lips caressed my ear. "All I want is for you to remember."

The lights stayed on, blaring a spotlight on a scene of us in his apartment shower. The sound of the steaming water beating our skin satisfied my senses. Looking through the glass at our naked bodies that fit together perfectly placed a weight on my heart. Pleasure filled moans escaped our lips and the sound of bliss mixed with the sound of running water and exited the shower walls to enter the space around us.

"What is this?" I shook my head at the wonderful memory, trying to keep it's temptation from affecting me.

"This is love." His whisper stroked my earlobe and I shuttered against my will. "This is a review of all that made me who I am in my life. And you're a huge part of that. Can't you see?"

"But..."

His warm hands snaked around my torso from behind, mimicking the way he held me in the shower. "Everything that's happening outside of this space cannot be changed. You're fighting a losing battle and I want to save you from the grief."

"You hurt me, Nolan." I shook my head. "You took my life in more ways than one."

"You're only hurting yourself trying to change the enviable." His hands were warm and comforting, luring me into the contentment I craved for so long.

The scene beneath the spotlight continued to change with every flicker. But now horrid and gruesome images of Nolan in various states of self-inflicted harm presented themselves. Flashes of bloodied forearms, oozing wrists, taught ropes with nooses, and the grizzly aftermath of unblinking bloodshot eyes, a mouth of pink foam, and an empty pill bottle.

"What is—" A gentle hand with delicate slender fingers caressed my chin, directing my sights from the horrid scene and into ocean blue eyes.

"That's proof that us being here together is meant to be. Fate." He smiled, emphasizing the deep dimples on his cheeks that I loved so much. "This will go on eternally until you accept it, like I had. And is being here together, making love and collapsing in each other's arms, so bad?"

"It feels ... good." I whispered and lay my head against his muscled chest. The comfort and pleasure drew me in with its familiarity. I wanted what we used to have. I wanted the laughter, the dimples, the warm embraces, the security.

"I love you, Rhea." Nolan ran his fingers through my hair. Not even the stickiness of my head wound stopped him from playing with the strands as he would after a night of ecstasy. "From now on, everything will be peachy. I promise."

"Peachy cobbler—" I paused and pressed my ear to his chest. The silence took me aback. "I don't hear your heartbeat."

"Heartbeats don't matter here." He continued caressing.

From somewhere deep in the blackness, the machine's beeping came through. Its rhythm matched the beat of my heart, which I could hear and feel pumping away in my chest. "You're wrong." I stepped back to separate our bodies, seeing the intense blue fade to black in Nolan's eyes.

"There's only this. This is all we have here. Each other." With each word that exited his lips, more of his dark, ghastly appearance began to reveal itself. His brow ridge slowly grew, causing his eyes and cheeks to sink in even more.

"If that's true, where is my life review?" I shook my head in disbelief, backing away ever so subtly. "You have your review because it's too late for you."

"You're confused." He shook his head, bringing attention to his matted and grimy strands of hair.

"You probably rewatch that review every time you die."

"You don't know what you're talking about."

"You died, Nolan. In every reiteration, no matter what changes, you die. But me? I'm still alive and I plan on keeping it that way."

He scoffed and glared as his forearms bled causing threads of blood to drip from his fingertips. "Not if I have any say over it."

**19**

**CHAPTER 19**

Familiar whimpering and soft sobs echoed from a faraway corner of the space, interrupting the nearby sounds of Nolan's ongoing life review. I ignored the scenes and the images within, purposely allowing those memories that included me to be background noise. I needed to find the source of the whimpering.

Even through the haunting, black fog, I needed to find my way back to Rhea.

I turned my back to Nolan, refusing to lay my eyes on the increasingly grotesque physical condition of the once handsome man I used to love. As the seconds passed, his appearance continued to take on the results of his many forms of death. Even as the stank of decay permeated the vicinity and sticky drips of dark, thick blood poured from the wounds on his forearms, I refused to look. What my memory captured was plenty and brutal enough to hammer into my mind.

My walking quickly transitioned to a jog, and then a sprint as I desperately put distance between us. I had expected him to be at my back or on my heels, but relief came over me when I realized he didn't follow.

The whimpering increased, letting me know I was moving in the right direction and getting closer to the source. My imagination made out the other Rhea on the white tiles, a trail of smeared blood behind her as she pulls herself to the main exit.

However, when a mysterious light ahead spotlighted an entirely different scene, it stopped me in my tracks.

There I was. The other Rhea, sitting alone on the living room floor of my mother's apartment. The comfy teal couch at Rhea's back looked inviting, but she refused to use it. Her hair looked like a bird's nest and her bare face was red and puffy from hours of crying.

"I know this," I whispered to myself. This was a year before starting my UpTube channel. I was a teen, suffering from an intense feeling of loneliness after Mom and Dad's separation. On her lap teetered a dogeared Carl Jung book filled with his psychological theories. I remembered doing a detailed report on him in high school. And then I realized, "Why am I seeing myself from high school?"

A chill came over me, and when I turned to confront the source, the light went out. It came back on like a flip of a switch, but this time before me in the spotlight was the other Rhea older than the previous by a couple of years. She contorted her body into several poses for the camera on the tripod. She did her hair and makeup like the popular female celebrities that were trending.

"I know this!" The familiarity of the scene brought on a sense of excitement. This was the time I was preparing to upload the video of fashion model poses that went viral and started off my career. I remembered the positive responses I received, the online friendships I made, and all the love. This one video took me from my sad, lonely existence and launched me to the well-known and much-loved fashion influencer of today.

I couldn't help but smile.

Again, the light went out, encompassing me in blackness. When the lights came back on, my eyes quickly adjusted to the other Rhea again. This time she was curled up in bed with the human sized white teddy bear with pink eyes Nolan had given me as a gift. What was the special occasion that prompted such a present? "You don't need a special occasion to enjoy gifts. You deserve all the things that bring a smile to your face," was Nolan's response when I had asked. But this occurred at the beginning of our relationship when he had to go away for business.

Again, there she was, alone and lonely, with hot tears streaming from her eyes to be blotted away and absorbed by the satin pillow. Just as her sobs shook her body, the light went out.

In the brief darkness, something occurred to me. Was this my life review? If it was, what did that mean for the other Rhea and for me?

The light came on, illuminating a scene that stopped me in my tracks. A handsome, clean-shaven Nolan with damp and messy hair atop his head. He had gotten out of the shower ten minutes ago and had thrown on a pair of pants before finding me in the kitchen of his home.

I stood in the shadows of the ethereal fog and watched as he walked up to the other Rhea and startled her at the bar counter where she sat. She laughed, giggling like the shy girl she wasn't, as he draped his muscular arms around her waist from behind.

"I thought you were going to bed." Rhea rocked on the stool, balancing as she clutched his forearms over her chest. Her form fitting black dress hugged her body and left her shoulders exposed with thin spaghetti straps.

"Not without you, beautiful." His British accent often came through when he spoke while smiling, and even now I had a difficult time ripping my gaze from his cheek dimples. "Couldn't stop thinking about you."

"Seems like every time you get naked, you think of me." She cocked her head back to investigate the blues of his eyes and he captured her lips in a kiss.

As I watched, partly reliving the moment, the memory made my heart sink. I remembered the love we had for each other, the admiration, the respect, and couldn't pinpoint the exact moment it all went sour.

Nolan pressed his chest to her back and pulled her to him by her hips. She laughed when he unbuttoned and unzipped his pants. "What are you doing?" Rhea asked with an all-knowing grin.

"I'm gonna show you how much you're on my mind." His teeth gently grazed the skin on her shoulder while his hands slid under her dress, easing it up over her thighs and hips.

I remembered the exact moment he ripped the lace panties because she yelped in surprise, but that surprise quickly turned to pleasure as he pulled her closer to the edge of the seat and guided himself into her from behind.

They both let out a pleasure-filled moan simultaneously. And I instantly relived the feeling of his hot chest against my back, especially as he guided the thin straps of the dress down over my shoulders.

She tossed her head back. Long, red hair draped their shoulders as his hips moved to a sweet rhythm only he was privy to. Still, in no time, her body undulated to his beat.

This scene had replayed a dozen times in my head following this night. One of the best moments he and I shared. Hot tears hovered on my lids as I watched them. He took care of me and fulfilled my every need. We were the source of each other's pleasure. How did it all go so wrong?

I turned my back to their lovemaking and their heavy, satisfied panting, awaiting the scene to change and highlight my tragic death. I expected turning around and seeing my handsome, beloved boyfriend crushing my head in and leaving me to die.

From a distant corner of space, Nolan's deep voice reached my ears. "I promise to make it like this forever if you promise to stay with me."

I shook my head and left the review behind, refusing to turn around, refusing to see what it was like when he placed me in a state of bliss. "You can't convince me I'm dead. I'm fighting for my life, and I'm not giving up. I won't fall for your bullshit, Nolan."

"I make the rules here." His voice grew louder, as if originating from the edge of space, like an all-powerful being. But I didn't let it stop me.

I was going to find the other Rhea and do all I could to get her out alive. This time, Nolan or his ghost wouldn't do anything to stop me. I wiped the hot tears from my cheeks with the back of my hand and continued walking, leaving the passion-filled moans and groans far behind me.

Then the slow beeping of the heart rate machine captured my attention. The mechanic beeping echoed from all areas of the space, bouncing around me, making it difficult to pinpoint exactly where it originated.

The only time I stopped walking was when the familiar beeping leveled out to one long beep. For a split second, my breaths caught due to fear.

I peered over my shoulder at the other Rhea and handsome Nolan while they continued making love. They had transitioned to Rhea sitting on the granite kitchen counter with her legs wrapped around Nolan's waist as he stood where the stool once was. They kissed like the insatiable lovers they were, moaning and panting into the kiss. Their hands explored every inch of flesh on their bodies, while they remained connected at the hips.

Annoyed, I shook my head, keeping my eyes on Rhea's blissful expressions. "You fool!" I shouted at her while making my way back to the sensual scene. "This is all he's ever given you. This is all he ever offered. How could you not see it? He never loved you. You mistook his gifts for caring, his sweet talk for respect, and his pleasure for love." Disgusted at her, at myself, I sneered.

Of course, she didn't respond, but Nolan broke the kiss to turn and look into my eyes. "You!" he growled when our eyes connected. His handsome face quickly distorted to the thick-browed, sunken black-eyed creature that roamed the ethereal space. "You bitch!"

I took in a sharp breath at the realization. "No." Surprised, my breathing increased with fear.

He approached, stepping over the threshold where the light of the scene met the foggy darkness. His naked body quickly changed from the healthy, fit specimen in the memory to one of death and decay. "You will stay because I will make you stay. You're mine. You belong to me."

This was no life review, but a trap. And I had stupidly become the fool in his game of manipulation.

As he marched toward me, I froze in a state of paralysis. Even the fog seemed to move away from him in fear.

My heart raced from the terror of him stomping his way toward me and the thought of what he would do once he had me in his grip. The racing heart in my chest confirmed I still had a chance to save the other Rhea. However, the gradual beep, beep reminded me of the ticking clock and time that was running out.

# 20

## CHAPTER 20

The gradual beeping sound chimed in my ears and ricocheted from invisible objects in the dark void surrounding me. I turned to run from the approaching ghostly form that had overtaken the beautiful naked body of the man I once loved, but before I could take a proper step, he had my forearm in his grip.

"You can't have me," I growled. "I was never yours to begin with and that's not changing now." I pulled my arm from his hold, the dark red blood on his palms acting in my favor. Even though he tried digging the tips of his fingers into my flesh, the pain didn't stop me from evading him.

I ran forward through the spacious blackness, following the vague beeping in the distance. I knew where the sound was leading me and had the urge to do nothing more than get there. A feeling in my gut told me once I reached the hospital room where my body lay, I would be safe even if respite would be brief.

Finally, the pinprick of light grew larger the closer I got and lit up the familiar scene. This time, my unconscious body wasn't alone in the bright hospital room.

The thinning red hair of the woman who stood over my body ushered in that sense of comfort I knew would meet me here. Her hair in a beat bun. Her broad shoulders resembled mine although they slumped with grief, and even so, I wanted to bury myself within those arms and rest on the nurturing shoulder.

"Mom?" I called. "Mama, it's me."

Of course, she didn't turn around. She couldn't hear me. She probably had no idea I was nearby, witnessing her eyes well up with tears and her lips tremble as she tried to get words out. "I'm so sorry, baby. I won't sleep until I do all that I can to find the person who just left you on the side of the road."

"What? No." I shook my head, trying to step foot over the threshold and enter the room. For some reason, no matter how much I walked or moved forward, the room evaded me, keeping me at arm's length. "No. A car didn't do that to me. It was Nolan, Mom. Nolan is at fault. He did this."

Why did her words seem so much like a goodbye?

She placed her warm hand on the forearm of my body, and I melded into her warmth, the softness of her fingers, the pressure of her grip. Tears blurred my vision as they fell over my lids like water from a broken dam.

I brought my arm up to confirm that I had indeed sensed her touch and was startled to see her standing at the bedside through my flesh. How could I forget I was fading and fast?

The light went out leaving me in darkness. "No!" I screamed, not ready to let the vision go. Only my sobs and sniffles were heard. The disappointment that darkness and not her arms enveloped me settled in. "Mama," I cried. "Don't leave me, Mama."

Suddenly, a feeling I had yet to experience washed over me. Defeat. I didn't want to do this anymore. I couldn't stand the fog, the dark, the loneliness. Maybe I fought so hard for nothing. Maybe

Nolan was right, and all my efforts were pointless. Fate had a plan and that plan had been put in motion and there was nothing I could do about it.

The proof was in the fact that this wasn't the first cycle I had encountered, yet I had made the same choices that led me to the same outcome.

I dropped to my knees, awaiting the inevitable to happen. Either Nolan would come swoop me up into his grotesques embrace or I'd simply fade away to be replaced by another phantom of me that would remain in this space with Nolan for eternity.

Then without warning, the light came back on, flooding me in utter whiteness until my sights adjusted to the large pool of blood and the trail smeared across the white tile floors of the photography studio. Throbbing in my temple increased and I whimpered in pain.

There, Rhea lay in a puddle of fresh blood, weak but barely conscious. Another spectral doppelgänger struggled to emerge from her back as she lay on her stomach, having collapsed during her attempt to crawl. From the looks of it, she was heading toward the door that led to the exit of the building.

To witness how hard she fought to get from the bedroom to the center of the spacious studio put a fire under me. How could I give up if she refused?

I stood making my way onto the scene with ease. When at her side I got down onto her level. "Rhea?" I waved my hand before her glazed over eyes as she stared through me and into space. She blinked slowly, bringing relief to my heart. Once fully aware, the struggling ghost at her back vanished, even if it was only temporarily. "Rhea, you can do this." I looked into her vacant eyes. "You need to keep going. Get to the door, that's all you have to do." I waved my hand in front of her again, burning my gaze into her until her eyes finally settled on me.

"Help me," she whispered and brought her palm to the horrid wound on her head. "I'm—I'm dying."

"No." I shook my head. "Not if I have anything to do with it."

She dismissed my doubt and sighed. "I'm bleeding out. Not gonna make it."

Right. What was I thinking? I had been too wrapped up in my own grievances to remember that we still had a chance. It might be slim, but Rhea still had a chance.

I got up to carefully make my way over and around the smeared and puddled blood that turned the once pristine room into a bloodbath. Although it probably couldn't affect me, being I was on a separate plane, subconsciously I tried to avoid it.

When I had to make my way past Nolan's lifeless body, I cautiously moved around him as he slumped in a pool of his own red liquid. Each step was calculated as I couldn't imagine walking through the stickiness. In my mind, I anticipated one of my careful steps being interrupted with a sudden grasp as he or his ghost reached out to stop me.

Thankfully the powers that be allowed me to move beyond his final resting spot and through the bedroom toward the bathroom. As I went into the claustrophobic space, I questioned why I was able to react with this scene and not the one with my body lying in the hospital bed.

There I was, in the bathroom. My aim was to search for a first aid kit with gauze or a hand towel I could take back to Rhea to help her stop the bleeding, but instead I was stuck looking into the mirror.

At first, nothing was there to greet me. The reflection I assumed would always be there was nowhere to be seen, but the more I focused the more I made out the recognizable eerie figures. Multiple images of me appeared, facing me but standing slightly behind the other. The visible parts of them and their wounds varied slightly.

When I shook my head in utter shock, they did too, mimicking me and my actions just as a reflection would.

I couldn't take anymore. I couldn't study the various injuries, bruises, and blood spatter on their faces and bodies. The thought of what it meant was too much for me to digest. I pivoted, placing my back to the mirror, and meeting the used hand towel hanging from the towel bar.

Reaching out to grasp it only brought my attention to my fading form and jumpstarted my sense of urgency. I lay my hand upon the white cloth, and just like the times before where I tried to interact with anything physical, my hand went straight through it.

"Damn it," I huffed in frustration. I remembered how I pushed the glass trophy, making it teeter on its base, and I took a deep breath. "Come on. I can do this. I need to do this for her. For me." Again, I placed my hand on the towel, feeling the soft fibers tickle my palm. "Yes, yes, yes." I pulled the cloth, and it slid over the metal rod and flopped onto the floor.

If I could perfect this and bring the towel to Rhea, maybe I could bring her the phone Nolan had hidden so she could call for help. If I gathered my strength soon, I could probably even open the front door and drag Rhea to the exit myself.

An optimism suddenly bubbled inside me. I crouched to get closer to the cloth and placed my fingers over it, preparing to pick it up. When a sound of a door latching, or unlatching stopped me in my tracks. I stood and turned to look behind me, fully anticipating ghost Nolan to be standing there.

When only the apartment and its contents were there, I frowned suspiciously. Although my heartrate had risen, I was left questioning. What had happened? I tried ignoring the searing throbbing in my skull, but it took far more effort than I could muster. I placed my hand to my temple, giving in to the pain and made my way back toward Nolan's body.

When I approached, I realized the sound I had heard was someone fumbling with the front door lock.

I rushed back into the studio where Rhea lay in same spot I had left her. When the front door finally opened, a relief washed over me when the bright light of the sun illuminated Joselyn in the doorway.

Euphoric excitement washed over me like a wave of warm water in the winter. "It's you, Jos! Yes, yes!"

She took only two steps inside before the door closed behind her. She gasped when her sights landed on the scene and dropped the bag from her hand, spilling its contents at her feet. "Rhea?!" Her high heels click-clacked as she rushed to Rhea's body. "Oh, my sweet Jesus. What happened to you, girlie?"

My heart raced in anticipation. "You gotta stop her bleeding, Jos." The words slipped out as if she could hear me, but I knew she didn't even know I was there.

Rhea removed her hand from her head wound and Jos gasped at the trauma of it. "What in the world happened to you? I need something. Uh, let me get you some kind of bandage." She kicked off her heels and rushed toward the back room. I stayed at Rhea's side as she struggled to push herself up with wobbly arms.

When a bloodcurdling scream came from the hall, I knew Jos had encountered Nolan's body. The way her screams tore through the space rattled the air around me and I covered my ears with my palm.

"What the hell, Rhea," she cried. "What the hell?"

It was silent for nearly a minute before Jos returned with the washcloth and a bottle of water her hand. This time, a shocked and vacant look nestled in her eyes. She slipped on a spot of blood, nearly falling but caught herself successfully. "What in god's bloody hell happened here?" She crouched, helping Rhea flip over to apply the cloth to her head to slow the bleeding.

After Jos assisted Rhea with a much-needed drink of water, she instructed Rhea to hold the cloth to her head. Some strands of her blond hair hung the back of her head instead of her loose ponytail, indicating she had moved quickly when gathering it up. I studied the contents that fell from her purse, as the makeup bottles and lip gloss littered the entry way but took note of the blank look in Jos's blue eyes.

An immediate question plagued me. Why hadn't she picked up her cell phone from among the litter of makeup to call for help?

# 21

## CHAPTER 21

From the ethereal space, I did the only thing I could do and watch as Joselyn assisted Rhea, holding the washcloth to her wounded temple. The white cloth quickly turned red as it became saturated with blood, and for a second, I thanked the powers that be for keeping her alive for as long as it had.

I closed my eyes and made a quick wish that we'd have enough time to get the help we needed.

Rhea's eyes remained closed, but I sensed her pain as we shared it. The intense pressure squeezed the circumference of my skull like a vice, and I wept for her. Out of curiosity, I placed my hand on my own temple, allowing my fingers to briefly examine and compare the wound.

"I'm dying." The words dribbled from Rhea's lips. "So tired."

I expected chaos and panic, but Jos just stared, pressing Rhea's hand to the washcloth to secure it against the wound. She refused to blink for several seconds as she took in the horrific sights around her. I, too, took in the contrast of bright red against stark white as the harsh spatters and smears painted the scene in utter terror. I knew the scene was enough to cause anyone to conquer some sort of shock.

How else would one describe the view? A crimson nightmare.

I crouched to get on their level, keeping my eyes locked onto Rhea's. "Tell Jos to call for help." When Rhea's bloodshot eyes landed on mine, I resorted to ghost Nolan's tactic and brought my fingers to my ear to mime answering a phone. "Tell her to call an ambulance or call someone, anyone to help." I emphasized help with my mouth.

Rhea's eyes narrowed in confusion. "My phone? Nolan has my phone."

I wondered if Rhea was communicating that info to me, thinking I didn't know, or to Jos to get her to act and find her phone or use her own. Either way, I glanced to Jos to see if she could snap out of it.

I couldn't determine what the look on Joselyn's face meant, what it conveyed. I wasn't sure if fright or shock was the only thing that seized her or what. It was hard to read, especially because I've never seen her out of her comfort zone. But as soon as she burst through that door, she was forced out of her element and thrust into a nightmare. She usually shimmied around with her bubbly attitude, lively, optimistic, and full of energy. She had always seemed willing to aid and assist, as that was part of her job title for years. It was as if aiding and assisting was not only part of her job or routine, but part of her DNA. But now I couldn't recognize her.

She followed Rhea's line of sight. "Who are you talking to?"

Rhea lifted a bloodstained finger to point to me. I looked back and forth from Rhea to Jos and stood, but Jos's eyes didn't follow as I had hoped.

"She..." Rhea started, moaning in pain. "She's helping me."

"Who's helping you?" Jos shook her head, looking straight through me. Her perfectly shaped eyebrows did somersaults as she searched the room with her eyes.

"My ghost." Rhea met my gaze. "Don't you see?"

Jos stood and with her eyes followed the trail of blood back to where Nolan's body lay. "Are you saying you killed Nolan and your ghost helped?"

I shook my head even though Jos couldn't see or hear me. "No, Joselyn. Listen to her."

"He tried to kill—" A coughing fit took the words right out of her mouth, so I tried to continue for her.

"Nolan did this to her, to us. He tried to kill me, Jos." I gestured to the wound, wishing she could see, hear, or somehow sense me. "Help her already! She's dying."

I hated seeing another version of me, my physical form, aware yet hunched over on the floor in pain and sitting in a mixture of Nolan's blood and her own, pressing a washcloth to an ugly, gaping gash on the side of her head.

Surreal couldn't even describe it.

But what had to be worse was standing around watching as my assistant and friend looked at her dying friend in shock and awe but not call for help.

"What is going on with you, Rhea?" Joselyn shook her head as a stream of tears streaked down her face, leaving streaks of dark brown eye makeup on her cheeks. "You killed him!"

"No, no." I shook my head and waved my hands around to protest.

"What happened, huh? You couldn't handle that he wanted to manage my career alongside yours?" She ran her hands over her face, wiping away the stream of tears. "I don't know why I even told you about that. I should've kept it to myself and just let him tell you when he was ready. Now you went and killed him."

"Jos, no." Rhea struggled with her words. "He...lashed out first."

"He texted me about a half hour ago," she went on. Her eyes changing shape from sad, nervous, and confused every second she talked. "It was as if he knew you were gonna attack him and wanted to name his killer."

"Wha—?" Rhea looked to me, begging, and pleading with her eyes. "No."

I had no idea what Jos was talking about but the look in Rhea's eyes told me I needed to do something, anything to help her. Had Nolan really texted her and made it look like Rhea tried to kill him unprovoked?

"I don't know what to do," Jos went on, this time pacing back in forth in front of Rhea. "What am I supposed to do?"

"Help," Rhea and I blurted out at the same time.

"But look at you." Jos shook her head. "You're insane, Rhea. You're seeing things. Ghosts that tell you to kill, and you want me to help you?"

While Joselyn went on, I rushed to the pile of items lying on the floor near the main door. Among the objects were lip gloss, a compact mirror, chewing gum and bottles of liquid foundation and nail polish that spilled from the small handbag. But what my eyes lingered on was Joselyn's cell phone.

It lay among the items screen down. The pink rhinestones on the protective case highlighted Joselyn's flashy personality and distinctly tied her to her property. I fell to my knees, getting as close to the phone as possible, extending my fingers to touch it. If she wasn't going to get it and call for help, maybe I'd do it myself.

Jos went on, her voice rising as her words tumbled from her lips. "I don't know what I'm supposed to do. I can't believe you killed Nolan. Did you beat him with that trophy? Is that what happened? I can only imagine what you would do to me."

"He hit me first," Rhea managed. She didn't even bother opening her eyes to speak.

"With your phone?" Jos went on, pacing back and forth, being careful to avoid the puddles of blood near her. "You already told me, but I thought you would have forgiven him by now. I didn't think once I leave you guys alone, you would go and bash his head in."

"No. You're ... not listening."

I wanted to scream to Jos again to listed to Rhea, but instead I ignored them and placed my sole focus on the phone just like I had the washcloth and the glass trophy before. This time the rigid plastic rhinestones were cold on my fingertips. The words, "You can do this," repeated over and over in my head as I pushed against the cold plastic to move the phone an inch.

"I knew you could do it," Rhea said, pointing to me. Had I been hearing her thoughts and words of encouragement that had somehow transported to my mind? "See? You, see?"

Jos didn't say a word she only stared at the phone. Had she seen it move? Maybe she was waiting to see what Rhea meant. Now was my chance to convince her. To show her that we were not crazy, and this was really happening.

Again, I placed my fingers against the phone and gave it a push that sent the phone sliding across the white tiles only to stop against Joselyn's foot.

She stared but refused to pick it up, taking a step back instead. "You got to be kidding me."

"See?" Rhea's breathing was labored. "Believe me... now?"

She placed her fingers to the thin blond hairs near her temple, closed her eyes and shook her head as if that action would cause her to wake up from a nightmare upon opening her eyes. When she opened them again, she stared directly at the phone. "No, this is ridiculous."

"The ghost is me," Rhea explained. "She was warning me. Nolan was dangerous."

I stood, getting Rhea's attention. "Is dangerous." Instinct told me to look around for any sign of his ghost as we mentioned him. I was afraid that even thinking his name would somehow conjure him. Wherever he was, he could stay there for all I cared.

Jos finally retrieved the cell phone and examined it cautiously. "I don't know what to believe anymore."

"Believe me," Rhea pleaded.

"Look at this and then tell me what you would believe." She tapped the screen of her phone before shoving it in Rhea's face. I approached to see the text message from Nolan. A cryptic message saying, "Rhea did it." Sent around thirty minutes ago. He must've sent it in the seconds before we ended him. "This doesn't sound like self-defense to me."

She had a point, but she had to give us the benefit of the doubt. She knew me. She should know I would never fatally hurt someone, especially the man I thought I loved, in cold blood.

When Rhea looked up at Jos, I knew exactly what was going through her mind. But she voiced it before I could. "You're gonna...let me die?"

"I—I don't know what to do." Jos threw her hands up.

"What kind of answer is that?" I shook my head, seeing the bullshit a mile away. "What's wrong with you, Jos? What have I ever done to you to deserve this?"

"Why?" Rhea panted, keeping eye contact. "Why, Jos?"

"All I ever wanted was to begin my acting career." She stared, and I no longer recognized the look in her eyes. Vacant. Distant. Empty. "He was my connection to the rest of my life, to my wish fulfillment, to my destiny. And you took that from me."

"You bitch!" I shouted, my voice echoing throughout the space but not strong enough to break through dimensions to affect her. The anger in me boiled and I channeled all my radiating pain and rushed to the scattered items on the floor. I kicked the bottles and the lip gloss in her direction. "You fake..." I kicked the compact, "selfish..." the mirror bounced from my shoe and soared through the air, "...bitch!" There went the pack of gum too.

I had always strived to be a good person, aware that my actions had reactions. And like the laws of karma required, I intended to express good so it would return to me. But even good girls had their breaking point.

Jos screamed as each item launched at her. She squirmed where she stood, dodging, and blocking most of the blows, but her wide, frightened eyes and screams were enough to satisfy my anger. "What's happening? What are you doing, Rhea?"

Rhea took in a deep breath. "She's pissed," she managed before collapsing to the tiles.

**22**

##### CHAPTER 22

A s Rhea collapsed to the floor, with the soaking red washcloth cushioning her head, I rushed to her side. Instead of touching her, my transparent hands were unable to shake her awake like I wanted them to do. At the realization of my limitations, my anger boiled into an intense rage that I had no control over.

I howled, releasing a fraction of my frustration. "What's wrong you?" I shouted at Jos, but she didn't react the way I anticipated. I wanted her to scream in fright upon hearing my voice and cry out upon seeing the heated anger in my phantom face, but unfortunately neither occurred. She only stared at Rhea's collapsed body, wide-eyed from shock. Her chest heaving from the seizing panic she seemed to suppress.

Even now, she refused to dial an ambulance or call for any help. And the thought of her phone resting in her palm, slowly draining its battery and becoming a useless hunk of glass and metal infuriated me.

"Rhea?" Joselyn's voice came out low and breathy. "I'm fucked, aren't I?" She pressed her hand to her heart and stared at her scattered possessions that littered the floor. "We all are. Am I right?"

She looked around the room. Was she looking for me? Was she talking to me in my ghostly state?

"What's the point now?" she went on. "Why even try when you're dying and Nolan's dead? I'm now part of it. Your fans will hate me. No one will hire me. What's the point?"

"What are you talking about, Jos?" I shook my head at her, the words seeping out through clenched teeth. "I can still make it. I can live if you help me. It's not over. It doesn't have to be the end."

"What's the point anymore?" She glanced back toward the grisly path of blood that led to Nolan's lifeless body. "What's the goddamn point?"

I sneered, watching her give-a-care meter drop before my eyes. "You coward."

"What's the fucking point, Rhea?" Her voice grew as she repeated the question as if she needed an answer. "Huh, you gonna answer me or what?"

She had been talking to me, the conscious, present, spectral form of the Rhea she knew. What did she expect me to say? It's better to be a half-ass hero than a selfish monster? I knew it was too late to convince her to do the right thing. I wasn't sure she recognized what the right thing was anymore, or even cared. The vacancy in her eyes told me her compassion and empathy had vanished along with her dreams of being an A-list actress.

She yelled again. "Answer me? I know you're here. I know you can hear me."

I stood from Rhea's side as she continued to lay laterally on the tiled floor. I moved toward Jos, only stopping when we stood nose to nose. Of course, she didn't react, which further infuriated me.

"If you were able to throw my stuff, you're able to talk to me," she went on. "Come on. Answer me."

All the pain and isolation I had kept pushed down and buried within for so many years, boiled to the surface. I couldn't keep it down even if I tried. I opened my mouth and allowed all my frustration spill out. "What's wrong with you, Jos? Get it the fuck together and pick up the phone. You've been by my side for how long, and suddenly that means nothing? You're just gonna let me die because of your nonexistent acting career?

"Or is this your way of punishing me because Nolan's no longer able to advance your dreams of acting?" I sneered at the tiny freckles on her nose as she peered over her shoulder toward Nolan's body. "You never cared about me, am I right? Just like Nolan. Being at my side was only a means to an end."

Joselyn's knees buckled and she bent to sit on the floor next to Rhea bringing her knees to her chest, not caring about what her fitted dress would expose. A stream of tears flowed down her cheeks while she rocked slightly and hugged her knees.

"No." I pointed an angry finger at her. "You're not allowed to sit and cry, damn it. Get the hell up and face what you've done."

Her sobs violently shook her shoulders, and her sniffles were muffled by the cuff of her elbow as she buried her face in her arm. But there was no mistaking her cries, her pain, possibly even a hint of regret as she folded into herself.

But strangely, just as sudden as her cries began, they abruptly stopped. An eerie silence settled around the space like the false sense of security from the eye of the storm. She sighed and stood, wiping the tears from her eyes. "I just came to check on Nolan after receiving a strange text from him and this is what I found, officer. I didn't call for help immediately because, because... I thought I could revive her. Yea, I tried to help." She nodded, reciting her lines like a scene from a script. "Yea, I tried to stop the bleeding, but it was too late."  She nodded again, content with the made-up narrative.

Intense rage bubbled within me like molten iron, and I released the fuming pressure with a guttural growl. "Arrgh!"

Joselyn's scream briefly startled me. And she back away from me, nearly falling to her ass on the floor. My intense gaze settled on her as my chest heaved from the release. Her eyes were now locked onto mine and it sent a satisfying warmth down my spine.

"How dare you?" The words tore from my throat so violently the pain in my head nearly incapacitated me, but I allowed it to fuel me instead.

"Rhea?" She took a few wobbly steps back.

"You're letting me die." The anger was like a drug, intoxicating me and influencing my next move.

"It's too late, Rhea." The fear in Jos's eyes satisfied something inside of me and I wanted more. "It's too late for all of us now. We're all screwed."

I growled again, and this time I felt my very foundation quake. Jos, too, looked around the room as if she felt the earth shudder before her gaze rested upon me again.

"Are you—you gonna hurt me?" she stuttered, her voice trembling with fear that exposed itself through her gawking eyes.

"As soon as I get my hands on you." I rushed forward, arms outstretched to sink my fingers into her flesh. I aimed for her shoulders, but my hands went straight through her, and momentum pulled the rest of through as well.

She gasped in shock which was quickly followed by a nervous chuckle upon realization. "You can't hurt me. I should've known." She cackled again. "You're probably nothing more than a figment of my imagination brought on by stress. Yes, I caught whatever Rhea had. That's all."

I tried to grip her shoulders again, but my translucent fingers passed right through her instead.

I let out an exhausted snarl before my worst nightmare appeared from beyond the brightly lit space of the studio. There, from the dark fog, emerged ghastly Nolan. Although he seemed to have the ability to change or manipulate his ethereal appearance, it seemed he preferred parading around as the grotesque beast he truly was. Valiantly flaunting his horrid state. The huge brow bone and hollow eyes sockets were the features that separated him from any recognizable human.

"Stay back," I demanded as he approached. But he ignored my request and continued to close the gap between us. Instead of backing away and cowering like he expected me to, I stood my ground. "Stay the fuck back, you psycho!" I pointed a threatening finger to send the message that I would fight forever if I had to.

As he continued toward me, his appearance grew softer, more handsome, and recognizable with each step. By the time inches separated us, his hair had fallen into the neat style I always admired, the light reflected the bright blue in his seductive eyes, and the thick dark liquid disappeared from his absent wounds.

Before I could question what was happening, he walked by without as much as a glance my way. His eyes and attention were fixed on something behind me. I turned to assess the scene realizing Jos had gone to Nolan's body to examine him, while ghost Nolan went directly to mine.

He kneeled next to my slumped form and gestured with his hand. As soon as he extended his palm, another red-headed phantom elevated from Rhea's body, sitting forward fully before languidly collapsing back to Rhea's exact position.

"No." My breath caught when I realized what he was trying to do. Out of instinct, I looked down over myself, lifting my arms to determine how time affected me. My breath caught in my throat as the tips of fingers were completed invisible. I felt them, sensed them, but no longer saw them.

"Come." Nolan coaxed the phantom again, extending his hand. She rose, taking on more color and density than me in my current form. "You can do it," he encouraged.

"Stop!" I kneeled to Rhea's side. "Nolan, please. Don't do this. Please, stop."

"Come to me," he insisted, disregarding my attempts, and speaking to the phantom who would soon replace me.

I waved my hand before Rhea's face, hoping she would open her eyes and see how urgent it was for her to remain conscious. "You have to get up, Rhea. You have to keep fighting."

Again, Nolan presented his hand, but this time the phantom struggled to rise. "Yes, you got it. You're almost here. Come to me, Rhea. Stop fighting it and give in. Let it take you. Let me take care of you."

"No!" I cried. "Rhea, wake up. You gotta get up. You may think it's easier to give up, but you have people who need you. Mom, I saw her. I saw the future and she's there with you. She has your back."

"Shut your filthy mouth." Nolan's attention had finally found me, and his growl startled me. "That woman is trash. She tried to ruin your life. She tried to ruin our happiness."

"That's not true. She tried to look out for me and warn me against the likes of you." I sneered.

He sneered back, his eyes quickly flickering between bright and blue to sunken and hollow. "If you continue this, you will regret it." His threat was enough to stop me in my tracks. I contemplated the possibilities, glancing to Jos who continued to mourn Nolan's body, unaware of the ethereal war that's been waged.

My attention went back to Rhea, her shallow breaths told me I had to practice what I preached and not give up on her either. We were one, and if she went down, it was up to me to get her back up.

"Rhea, listen to me. Mama loves you and will do anything to see you again. You have to get up. If not for anything else, do it for her."

The phantom at her back collapsed and disappeared just as Rhea opened her eyes to look directly at me. I waved my hand, signaling her to get up, but Nolan stood before she could even try. He towered above us both.

"Mom," Rhea mumbled. "Mama."

His hollowed eyes released a dark red liquid that dripped down his face. "The sooner you're gone, the faster I can have what I want. And I'm tired of playing games. Now it's time for you to say goodbye for good."

**23**

### CHAPTER 23

As Rhea outstretched her arm, reaching for something that wasn't there, she continued to mumble, "Mama." Laying on her side, weak and in need of assistance, she groaned, and I could see death closing in even without the decelerating beeping of the vital sign monitor in the distance.

A pit formed in my heart for her suffering, for our pain. But I didn't have time to bemoan as Nolan towered above her with a menacing glare in his leaking, hollow eyes like a giant to an injured young lamb. The way his body levitated inches above the ground, the toes of his shoes angled straight down in the most unnatural way, sent chills down my spine.

"You are no longer needed." He moved toward me, not even an attempt to lift a foot to step over Rhea who lay on the floor in her own blood, his legs easily passed through her as if her body was nothing more than an illusion. And he treated her as such, showing no interest in the physical body whatsoever. "I'm gonna get rid of you once and for all."

"You would have tried to get rid of me even before this runway gig if I had the courage to use my voice back then and tell you to fuck off." Although I backed away to keep space between us, I mimicked his glare, keeping my eyes locked on his grotesque facial features. I wanted to dig deeper, to pull from my pain and really hit him where it hurt. "I should have listened to my mom a long time ago and left you alone to rot in hell."

He hissed from the stink. "You wouldn't have left me. I gave you your career," he countered. "You're a smart girl, babe. You followed the money, fame, and success. I could have battered you black and blue and you would have stayed, because I made you who you are. That's no secret."

"I was unhappy. No, miserable." I went on, taking deliberate steps back that took me further from Rhea. In case her conscious slipped again, Nolan would be nowhere near her to coax the other phantom to stay. "I told you everything was fine, made you believe I was content, and that things were peachy cobbler. But now I realize I was trying to convince myself of those things. I was broken. We were broken. And we both know the lie we lived."

"Broken things exist to be fixed," he continued toward me. "I am an expert and repairing broken things. That's why you hired me, that's why you fell in love, that's why you let me inside of you. Because I fixed you, your sad life, and your lackluster career. I made you, Rhea."

I nodded, agreeing. "Sure. You're right. You can take credit for it all—my happiness, my life, my career—but what good is any of it now anyway?" I went on. "Look at me, even if I survive this, I will never be the same. You made sure of that. No one will want to hire me, photograph me, or see me in a beauty campaign ever again. And you know what? I like it that way. So, go ahead and take credit for my entire existence as Rhea, but the one thing you won't take is my life."

"Ma?" Rhea's muffled voice grabbed my attention as she cried, "Mama?"

Jos appeared from my periphery, cautiously making her way towards the horrid scene. "Rhea?" she called out, her voice soft yet shaky. "Can you hear me?" There was concern in her demeanor but not for the right reasons.

"Ma?" Rhea managed, but this time her cries registered. The entire time she had been calling out to Mom but reaching out to me. She must have been confused, mistaken me for Mom and begging for my help. It must have been heartbreaking watching who she thought was her mother back away from her during a pivotal life or death moment, when a daughter needed her mother the most.

As Jos and I kept our gazes on her, Nolan grew curious and turned to look as well. I took the opportunity to extend my arm to her to encourage her not to give up.

Jos kneeled beside her, a mixture of curiosity and worry in her demeanor. "What about your mom, Rhea?"

The talk of Mom brought up a memory of the recent conversation Jos and I had while we were in this very room discussing my mother. A moment of bonding I thought would allow me to embrace being vulnerable and let my guard down around a person I foolishly believed cared about me.

Earlier, right after Jos spilled the news about Nolan managing her acting career, the conversation had transitioned to my mother and how she had told me my high school bully hurt me because he secretly loved me.

That conversation triggered a memory.

"A few years ago, my mom would schedule a date and time to come see me and I would set an alarm on my phone to remind me."

My phone!

I needed to get to my phone.

My eyes immediately locked onto the open door that led to the apartment and the bedroom. Nolan had hidden the phone under the mattress of the bed, and now my sole intent was to get to it.

While Rhea unintentionally kept Nolan and Jos distracted, I rushed toward the apartment and immediate made my way to the area on the bed where I remember Nolan hiding my phone. I knew it was there, even though I couldn't see it. I extended my hand to touch the mattress, and unsurprisingly my fingers went straight through.

There were times where I thought about the existence of poltergeists and if they truly had the ability to disrupt electrical currents and move heavy objects around the room like they were depicted in movies. If I had the ability to push a glass trophy, move a hand towel, and kick solid items while in this ghostly form, I knew I could manipulate a cell phone as well.

But I didn't have enough time to prepare, because Nolan's bony fingers clenched my arm and pulled me from the mattress.

His frustrated growl rang in my ears. "Why won't you die already?"

"Go to hell," I countered. And rushed to the mattress again. This time I placed my sole intention on finding the phone, imaging it sandwiched between the pillowtop mattress and its box spring. As my hand sunk into the corner of the bed, my fingers grazed something hard and smooth. Adrenaline kicked up a flurry of excitement in me that was immediately snuffed out by Nolan's tight fists in my hair.

He yanked me back and I splay out flat staring up at nothingness. Even the dark fog on the ethereal edge of the dimly lit room swooshed in spirals from the force of his pull. His hands remained tangled in my strands, and out of instinct I gripped his bloody wrists as he dragged me along the floor and away from the bed.

I screamed from the pain that radiated from my head wound, and the ornate light above the bed and the lamp on the nightstand flickered.

The way his fingers curled and twisted in the tangles caused my head to ache as chunks of hair were ripped from my scalp. Before I could think of my next move, I kept hold of his wrists as he lifted me by my hair and slammed my body back to the floor. For my skull to meet the hard tile was his intention, but I reached up on his forearms and dug my fingers into his lengthy open wounds to thwart his plan. My fingers sunk into his flesh like cold, wet clay as I wanted nothing more than to redirect my pain onto him.

His howling cries pierced my eardrums as they existed his mouth and echoed from every direction surrounding us. The lights continued to flicker out of sync, and he finally released his hold.

With the remnants of his old clumps of blood on my hands, and despite the transparency of my fingers, I pushed myself up to my feet to sprint toward the bed. Without looking back, I reached inside the mattress until the cold glass and metal registered on my skin.

Not sure how to proceed I allowed my need to quickly guide me. All I could think of was Mom and how much I wanted to be in her comforting embrace, and if I would ever get that chance again. With my fingers on the phone and the thought of Mom in my mind and heart, the phone startled me when it did what I envisioned and began to chime.

"How did you—?" Nolan grunted. "What did you do?"

My eyes widen in exhilaration. I've done it. I somehow made the alarm go off, and its high-pitched jingle was music to my ears.

"Turn it off," Nolan ordered. "Or I won't only get rid of you. I will make you suffer before I do."

My head throbbed but I ignored it, gritting my teeth in the process. "If you want it off, do it yourself." I ran toward the open door that led to the studio and glanced over my should when I realized he wasn't following.

Instead, he knelt near the corner of the bed and swiped at the mattress with his bloody arms. Every attempt and every swipe went right through the bed as well but didn't stop trying.

No wonder he had communicated to his handsome counterpart through body language only. Maybe body language was his only means of communicating and interacting with physical space. Although it seemed he had many possibilities to master terrorizing me in this ethereal realm, he had yet to master manipulating physical objects.

I left him near the bed and continued through the door toward Rhea and Jos. At first, I thought Joselyn had her eye on me as I entered the room, but she had only been looking in the direction of the room instead. "What's that? A phone?"

I glared into her wide eyes and envisioned tangling my fingers around that dirty blond ponytail and yanking her to the floor like Nolan had done to me. Always the good girl, I would never, in any circumstance, leave her to slowly die if the tables were turned. And that betrayal roaring inside me brought out and anger I wasn't sure I could contain or wanted to.

Jos dropped to Rhea's side, balancing on her knees. "Hey, is that your phone?" She tried desperately to get Rhea's attention.

Rhea looked beyond her and at me.

Standing only feet away, I nodded. "Yes, tell her. Tell her it's your phone." I pointed and nodded, trying my best to communicate nonverbally.

Rhea sighed. "Yes. Please. Jos."

The look in Joselyn's eyes conveyed a worry that wasn't for Rhea and her wellbeing, but a fear I had yet to witness. "What's the alarm for?"

Rhea lifted her arm to me as if asking me to grab it, to save her from the fear and pain. "Mom." In her weakened state she must have confused my hair, slender frame, and broad shoulders with Mom's. I couldn't blame her, genetically Mom was part responsible for my sought-after look.

Jos glanced over her shoulder towards me. Her hair swung with the sudden jerk, but her eyes looked right through me. "Mom? What does that mean?"

"Mama," Rhea said with a wearied sigh.

And the realization finally hit Joselyn, causing her to gasp. "The alarm. You set your alarm when she says she's coming, but she never does. Your mom, you're not planning for her to come over, right?"

Before I could let Rhea muster up another word, I nodded excitedly. "Yes. Tell her yes."

Rhea mimicked me with a nod. "Mom's coming."

"What, no." The panic caused her voice to crack. "You can't be serious. What have I done? What the hell did I get myself into?" She paced before me. "What do I do? Oh, my gosh. How do I fix this?" She seemed to be talking to herself more than anything.

Rhea groaned. "Help."

The alarm continued to chime from the other room as Jos shook her head. "It's too late for that. I'd really be ruined if anyone came here now. Fuck! The headline. I already know the headline. 'The assistant to the internet's beloved fashion influencer revealed to refuse to help upon finding Rhea near death.'"

"No." Rhea moaned. "I won't tell."

Frustrated grunts sounded from the bedroom, but I was the only one to react to them, turning to look. I could only imagine Nolan trying everything in his power to retrieve the phone and stop its chiming.

**24**

# CHAPTER 24

From far at the edge of the foggy space, the languid beep, beep of the hospital monitor melded with the chime of the phone alarm.

Joselyn watched the doorway. Her eyes wide from fright as if she was expecting the devil himself to emerge. "Your mom can't come here. Not now. If anyone sees me here like this—"

Rhea didn't respond. In fact, she didn't say or do anything. Her eyes glazed over as they landed on mine. A faraway stare that unnerved me and sent a shiver down my spine.

"Rhea?" I knelt beside her, trying to get her to move or say anything. I waved my hand before her eyes. "Hey, you can't give up. We have to get you out of here."

Joselyn crept toward the apartment where the phone's alarm called to her like a siren of the sea. Her apprehension to rush into the room revealed how uncomfortable and scared she was of what she might find once she entered.

Rhea remained on the floor, staring, unblinking. Her hair matted and caked with dark thick blood. Her once bronze complexion now taken on a pale grey hue. The thought that in this moment she could take her last breath, blink her final blink, and leave what would be left of her to Nolan, caused anxiety to grip me in my gut. But the faint mechanical beeping lit a fire under me. I had to do something. Anything. I couldn't allow this to be the end.

"Get up," I ordered. I waved my hand and snapped my fingers, gesturing for her to react and take action. "You have to get up and get to the door."

She only lay there, eyes locked onto mine, unblinking.

Anticipating the final phantom emerging from her body, I reached out to jostle some fight into her but stopped short when I couldn't see my entire forearm. It not only become transparent, but even the faint outline had disappeared. Alarmed, I lifted both arms to quickly determine the progression. As I feared, more and more of me was disappearing into nothingness. Thank goodness I still had my sense of touch, as I reached out to paw her shoulder.

With an eager intent of connecting, my fingers gingerly grazed her dewy skin and her eyes widened, startling us both. She felt my touch and I felt her too. Her arm was cold and clammy, even the spot that was free from blood.

"Mom?" she whispered, her soft voice was separate from the beeping, chiming, and frustrated grunts that filled the space around me. "Mama?" She narrowed her eyes as if to get a better look.

"No." I shook my head and pointed to her and the front door. "I'm you and we're gonna get you out of here." I signaled for her to get up.

She struggled, pushing herself up on her hands and knees. As she paused to gather her strength, the fingers of her right hand rhythmically tapped the tiles, making me realize I too had been unknowingly tapping my fingertips along my thigh. Anxiety of the unknown, the pressure to succeed, and the fear of failing needed an outlet when I was hellbent on suppressing those feelings.

It all made sense now and it only took me seeing my life from another point of view to give me perspective.

Rhea grunted though the pain and exhaustion as she moved forward.

"Yes, yes," I encouraged. "Get up, Rhea. Get up now and get to the door. You have to hurry."

She crawled, one arm and leg before the other. Pushing herself to clear just a few feet. I knew the pain that threatened to beat her down, I felt it too. The spasming pressure around my head, the icy tiles and tacky blood on her hands, the clammy dew along her forehead and neck. Even the weight of her body bearing down on her knees was excruciating when you wanted to give up the fight and rest. I understood her pain but giving up was not an option.

"Come on, Rhea," I cheered through clenched teeth. "You can do this."

She tried to stand but wobbled and collapsed back to the floor. Out of frustration and urgency, I slipped my hand in the crease of her elbow, feeling the muscle tense with shock.

"Wha—?" She locked eyes with me.

I nodded, reassuring. "I've got you."

She mimicked me and nodded and pushed herself to stand with my help.

As she managed to move a few feet toward the front door, it occurred to me that we would need the keycard to unlock it. Nolan, being the self-proclaimed protector, made sure only those suitable could access the studio. That being him, Jos, and me. Although he hadn't given me a keycard and kept his in his possession. I had no idea where his could be. However, Jos always had her keycard on her, and I knew exactly where she kept it.

My gaze landed on her handbag toppled over on the floor where she dropped it. The name brand purse remained open and abandoned along with most of its items. I motioned to Rhea to wait by putting a finger up. She nodded and tried to balance on her own while I left her side to go to the purse.

Getting low to the ground, I peered inside the handbag. Recognizing the distinct thin and rounded corner of the black keycard. When I reached inside to retrieve it a foot came down on it, pinning my hand to the ground. When I looked up, Nolan's evil features stared back.

"Looks like someone's being a naughty girl." He beamed the vilest, overextended grin I had ever seen. "Naughty girls deserve to be punished."

His shoes crushed my fingers against the tile as if he were stomping out the butt of a lit cigarette. I cried out from the pain and pulled my hand back, glad that I brought the key card with it.

The coldness of the thin card between my fingertips gave me the confidence I needed to continue fighting. There was no doubting that I could do this. I had the ability to help Rhea get out of this building and far away from the threats that tried containing her, but first I had to keep Nolan from stopping me.

While the phone's alarm provided a great distraction for Joselyn, it was apparent Nolan had given up trying to turn it off. The dripping, black ooze from his eye sockets stole my attention and preventing me from looking away. "We're getting out of here, Nolan. So, you might as well step aside."

"Why step aside when I can do this?" He floated directly toward me, tips of his shoes just skimming the floor.

I backed away, getting closer to Rhea whose eyes were fixed on the keycard that must've been oddly floating in thin air from her perspective.

The more I tried to keep a safe distance between us, the further from the door I got, which was probably part of his plan.

"It's over." I threw my hands up in defeat. "Just give up already."

"Using my words against me, huh?" He continued my way. "When have I ever given up, Babe? Nothing's ever stopped me from getting what I want. And neither will you."

In a blink of an eye, his hand was around my neck, pausing me in my tracks and causing me to drop the keycard. The agony of his thumb digging into the flesh at my voice box plunged me to my knees. My hands tried to break his grip, but the thought of him winning overcome and weakened me.

I dug my fingers into the wounds on his forearms again and he only growled, not letting me go like I had hoped. A fire raged in my lungs, and I grew desperate for a breath of air. With my head back, I pummeled, kicked, and scratched.

My eyes widened to take in the bright exhibit lights on the ceiling that flickered and flashed out of sync. For a moment the beauty of the lights mesmerized me, and I wanted to relax and stare at them forever. The rhythmic flashes attempted to lull me to sleep, but they soon matched the slow beeping that acted much better than the phone's alarm at keeping me attentive.

The look on his twisted face was nothing short of content. For a moment I wondered how many times during our relationship had he fantasied about this very moment. Silencing me with a dominating grip on my neck.

The beeping pulled me back to the matter at hand and I once again returned to his long, gruesome wounds on his forearms. This time I didn't stop at sinking my fingers in, I continued with a pull and rip, removing chunks of cold, wet pulp.

His howling shook the room, and he finally released me.

I choked on my words as I pushed myself to stand. "I'm leaving."

"You're not."

"Yes, I am." I coughed, clearing my throat, and catching a breath. "I'm fucking leaving like I should've done long time ago. You're going to hell and you're not taking me with you."

"You leave the way I want you to. When I want you to."

I shook my head, taking his words from earlier and twisting it on its head. "I'm gonna disappear from you the same way your parents did, grab the key and walk right out of the door, never looking back."

He cocked his head. "You...bitch. You know how much I despise you bringing them up." He growled and ran his thumb across his neck, indicating what he intended to do to me.

From behind him, Joselyn entered the room with my phone in her palm. She paused when she saw Rhea standing in the middle of the studio with the keycard in hand. But before I could do or say anything, the entire space went utter black, and a spotlight flashed on illuminating the spot where Jos had been standing.

Now, instead of her standing there wide-eyed, the man and woman from Nolan's life review was there. The anger and disappointment on their faces said enough.

"This is what you've given up your life for?" The woman glared at me in distain although it was apparent her words were to Nolan, her son. "This is how you chose to ruin your existence?"

"We're disappointed in you, Nolan." The man lengthened his back, broadening his shoulders. "Some son we got here, huh?"

The woman shook her head in disapproval.

"Get out of here!" Nolan swiped the air as if they would disappear in the surrounding fog, but they remained. Staring, watching, shaking their head in unison. "Leave. Go. Get gone, won't you?" he demanded but they refused.

Back and forth their heads rocked on their shoulders, side to side, sneers on their judgmental faces.

"Leave me alone," he cried, shoulders slumping like a little boy being punished. "Just leave me already." His father was first to turn, and his mother followed. "Wha—wait."

Together, side by side, they took a step into the fog. Before the darkness could completely consume them, Nolan rushed after them. "Wait!" he called out. "I didn't mean it." He went chased them until they all were one with the swirling mist.

The light crept in, slowly revealing the studio and Jos trying to wrestle the keycard from Rhea. "Give me the key and I'll give you the phone."

"Don't believe you," Rhea managed.

Jos wouldn't let go of the keycard. "All you have to do it text your mom not to come and then I'll let you go."

"Stop!" I screamed, and the lights flickered, hindering Jos. "Leave her alone," I cried out and Jos's sights landed directly on me.

"Oh, my god." Her eyes were so wide they seemed to pop out of her head.

I channeled the fed-up beast within and growled, sprinting toward Jos. She screamed and put her hands up over her face in defense. I let out my frustration and anger by throwing all my strength into her, knocking her off her feet and to the floor so hard her body slid a few feet on the messy tile. "Leave us alone."

I rushed to Rhea's side and concentrated on helping her up. The silence in the space alarmed me, although Jos's whimpering occasionally cut through it. The lights continued to flicker as I pulled Rhea to the front door. I glanced over my shoulder to see Jos standing and preparing to pounce.

I turned to Rhea and we both looked into each other's eye. "You have to run. Don't stop running until you find help. You hear me?"

She nodded and together we placed the keycard against the reader and the door unlocked.

Jos approached apprehensively. "Wait, Rhea. Just ... one second."

I gripped the door handle and pulled until the blinding sunlight hit us like the light a spotlight on a stage, giving us one last chance to give the audience a proper send off.

"People!" Rhea pointed to something in the distance.

I peered through the glaring light, but I didn't see people, I saw myself in the hospital bed. The exposed parts of my body were so transparent I could see the bottom bed sheet through them.

Jos reached out. "Rhea, wait."

I nudged Rhea, prodding her over the threshold. "Run!"

She did. She rushed through the door and out into the white light, and I didn't wait a second running too. Side by side, in the blinding light, our pace matched, and I couldn't be prouder that she was giving it all she had.

Running nonstop the hospital bed seemed to get closer, closer, closer. I anticipated finally getting away from the dark hellscape and getting back to my body. Only feet away I continued running alongside my counterpart. "Yes!" My feet carried me, bringing me to the edge of the space.

From right behind, Nolan's familiar voice sent a shockwave through my system. "Don't do this, Rhea. Stay—"

With death at my doorstep, I had to muster up the courage to do what seemed impossible. With all my strength, I took a breath, ignored the searing pain in my temple, and took a leap, landing on the bed just as I heard the squeal of car tires and a blaring car horn.

The sound of impact was the last thing to enter my ears before everything went black.

## 25

## CHAPTER 25

"Eyes wide open." The ethereal echo bounced around my surroundings, coming from somewhere far away yet nearby. The familiar tone of Nolan's masculine accent rattled around inside my head, yet blackness enveloped me in its icy embrace. I searched the darkness, struggling to see something, anything, that could act as my anchor.

Finally, blinding light stung my vision as my eyes snapped open to the recognizable hospital room. I now lay in the exact hospital bed I had seen in the astral plane and confusion hit me just as hard as the intense brightness. My senses adjusted to vivid florescent lights, the surrounding display of posters on stands and flowers in decorative vases, and that abrasive mechanical beeping next to me.

I turned my head to view the numbers on the vital machine, unaware of what any of the numerals meant. But I took note that this time the beeping was steady and robust unlike before, but it still rattled in my ears. Trying to get my bearings, I took in my surroundings, studying the dozens of fan-made prints, cards, and containers of flowers that crowded the unoccupied spaces of the small space.

The art and drawings varied in quality on the oversized get-well cards signed by many of the young women that called me their role model, inspiration, and aspired to be just like me. Some of their art drawn in pencil detailed majestic scenes of Nolan and his handsome bedroom eyes, holding me in his oversized, angelic-like wings. They had captioned other artistic renderings in the hashtag #RhelanNoMore, and even fewer mentioned Nolan at all.

The pain in my skull demanded my attention, and I reached up to examine the bandage wrapped around my head and questioned how long my body had been lying here since witnessing it from the other side.

I recalled first being frightened of the phantom that strangely looked like me, being in her body while navigating through the rehashing of the horrific experience of being brutality attacked by the man I loved. Just the thought of the diamond shaped glass trophy was enough to relive the horrifying moments over and over again in my head.

And worst of all, I had been forced to experience that very moment repeatedly from both perspectives, as a victim and a phantom witness. Both viewpoints would forever wound me far beyond the physical.

The last memory of my ghostly body nearly fading into nothingness hit me when the monitor's beeping reminded me of the warning of time quickly passing. The sudden fear of disappearing into nonexistence flooded my mind, and I lifted my hands to examine them, too. Counting each of my fingers repeatedly, I thanked the heavens they were no longer transparent and I was back in my physical body.

Even while lying in bed, the weight of my body sinking into the mattress brought on a physical, weighty sensation I had to become used to. I tried to lift my upper half from the mattress, hoping to sit forward and get a better look at the condition of my body, but decided against it after a sharp pain shot through my torso. Exhaustion washed over me at the thought of any exertion. I continued to lie in bed and scanned the room with my eyes instead, recognizing the elongated crystal vase with long-stemmed red roses extending from the top of it.

For a minute, my heart skipped at the thought of the giver of the roses. A memory from long ago of Nolan walking through the door of our home with two dozen of those same roses nearly made me jump out of my skin at the thought of him being alive and invading the privacy of my room. But just as the memory faded, so did the anxiety that ran through me, especially when I realized Nolan was now gone forever.

He would never walk into my room or my life again, considering what I had to do to escape with mine. Flashes of the hefty trophy coming down on his head, similar to what he'd done to mine, flickered in my mind. The frightened look on his face just as he put his hand up to stop me. That look in his eyes would forever replay in my nightmares but would be endurable over reliving the brutality of what he'd done to me.

The handsome man of my life.

The attractive man of my fantasies.

The man of my dreams.

My eyes never left the roses. One of the rose heads had a few of the petals picked off the way I remembered Jos was about to do during the vision. She had really visited. For a second, all my memories blended with one another, and I wasn't sure if the recollections were mine as myself or the ghost, but I was sure they weren't part of my imagination. I felt how real those visions were and knew, as a phantom, I had truly visited my body in the hospital.

Would anyone else believe me? Probably not, but either way I wanted proof.

I continued taking in the sights, looking for anything out of place, when a small, folded piece of white paper at the foot of my bed caught my eye. I wouldn't have even thought to look if it wasn't for the memory of her visiting, which was the proof I needed.

The torn sliver of paper barely hung onto the edge of the sheet and one wrong move would send it cascading to the floor.

Despite the pain, I pushed myself up in bed, taking a brief pause to orient myself and allow some of my aching to ease. The soreness wasn't only in my torso and around my head, as I had mistakenly thought, it was throughout my entire body. My ribs, hips, and knees throbbed especially along my left side.

I pushed through the pain and reached down toward the paper. My fingernail grazed the edge, and I held my breath to push myself a millimeter more and pluck the piece of paper from the sheet with the tips of my fingers.

I lay back slowly, inhaling steadily, noting the machine and the uneven beeping it produced. When I finally relaxed in a manageable position, I unfolded the scrap and the words hit me in the gut.

Mention her fans missing her. Tell her I miss her, and Nolan misses her, too. Bring up the car accident. Don't forget this line: "This world is so fucked. But don't worry, I'm sure Nolan's looking down at you, giving you the strength to pull through and fully recover."

I looked up from the note to meet the lens of a security camera affixed to the ceiling in the room's corner, watching, and possibly recording, everything. There was no doubt Joselyn would have made a brilliant actress, if only she didn't keep scripts and pointers on her person to fall from her pocket, get misplaced, and end up in the wrong hands. I tucked the paper in my fist, clinging to it for the evidence I needed to make sure Joselyn wouldn't get away with her part in my predicament.

The white board on the wall across from me displayed the room's number, my assigned doctor, and today's date. I nearly gasped at the number of days that had passed.

I needed answers. Where was Jos? Would Mom return to visit again? What did the public know and what would come of it?

Thankfully, before I could relax completely, the door to my room opened and a handsome older man wearing a grey button-down shirt and dress pants marched in, immediately followed by two nurses in matching light green medical scrubs. My eyes quickly connected with the couple of uniformed police officers that trailed behind them.

The short, dark-skinned policewoman had the energy of a leader. She moved past the tall fair skinned police officer and made her way to the front of the pack, standing to the side of the bed and apart from the others.

I expected her to speak first, but the well-dressed man with a clean-shaven warm smile began. "Good evening. How are you feeling?" I shook my head, cutting my eye back to the policewoman, and he continued. "I'm Dr. Shaw. Joining me is a couple of nurses, and this is the county's police officers who'd like to speak with you."

"Hello, ma'am," the policewoman finally spoke, forcing a smile through the concern that appeared in her dipped eyebrows.

The doctor cleared his throat, taking center stage. "I'd like to conduct a simple assessment before you two continue if you don't mind. Can you tell me your name?" He paused, awaiting my answer, and all eyes were on me.

"Rhea Patel."

"Good." He nodded. "Do you know where you're at?" I pointed to the whiteboard that contained that information. "Good, good. Do you know why you're here?"

"He attacked me." My eyes went to the policewoman to judge her reaction, but movement at the open door caught my attention. The head that peeked through the narrow gap filled me with a sense of ease, as it was the only person I'd recognized. "Dr. Desiree?"

Her thin lips curved into a smile and waved by twiddling her fingers, a mixture of sadness and relief in her glossy eyes. "Glad to see you."

I shook my head in confusion. "Why are you here?"

"Your assistant reached out to me to inform me of the accident and request I send your medical records here for the doctors treating you. I wanted to check in as your primary and as a friend."

"Ms. Patel?" The policewoman cut in. "Being that you're a high-risk patient and an internet sensation, they have stationed us outside of your room door, hoping to speak with you for a while. See, we've been trying to piece together what happen that resulted in you being hospitalized. What can you recall about how you sustained your injuries?"

"Nolan attacked me." I glanced around at all the unresponsive eyes. "Nolan Hudson, my boyfriend-manager."

"So, you know that your lover, uh, Nolan, is no longer with us?"

"I know. He's dead." Surprisingly, my lips quivered as the words left my lips. The reality of his death, and the fact that I caused it, hit me harder upon speaking it aloud.

"There wasn't a break-in at the studio?" the other officer asked. "An attempted robbery for valuables, your UpTube trophy?"

How did they come up with that scenario?

"No." I shook my head. "Nolan used that trophy to attack me. And then I used it to defend myself."

The unease in the room quickly escalated as the officer pulled out a notepad and the others glanced at each other in surprise.

"Your assistant, Joselyn Murphy," the policewoman continued. "In her report, she states she believes someone had stolen her keycard and entered the studio to steal valuables. Your lover possibly tried to stop the robbery and lost his life, leaving you to be attacked by the intruder. After following the intruder out of the building, they hit you with their vehicle as you tried to escape." She paused, an unnerving silence. "So, you're telling me that's not what happened?"

"No." I glanced at Desiree, searching for a sense of familiarity to help ease my anxiety. "No one took my lover from me during some heroic act. He tried to kill me, so I removed him from my life by taking his."

She nodded, as if the pieces were finally coming together. "And what about your assistant?"

"She showed up after he died, but instead of getting help for me, she wanted me to die, too." I threw the wad of paper back where I found it at my feet, grunting from the pain in my side. I nodded to the scrap, encouraging the officer to pick it up. "That's

Jos's handwriting. I'm sure you can check the camera recordings to see when she dropped this."

I almost ignored the creative posters acting as a barricade, keeping me inside this small, lonely space. I finally understood the story they were telling. Much of the art showed that public speculation was exactly what the officers were questioning. Many believed a crazed UpTube fan had assaulted me and Nolan and left Nolan dead, and when I ran to get away, they hit me with their car before fleeing the scene.

What they didn't know was all that was a lie orchestrated by Joselyn to protect her. She probably didn't expect me to awaken and tell the world the truth.

I wondered how my young female fans would take knowing that my fairytale life was that of the dark and grim kind. No matter how much I gave to him or loved him, my Prince Charming turned out to be The Big Bad Wolf in disguise. And I could never change that about him, no matter how many chances I had.

Wealth, fame, and heroism made the perfect fairytale ending. Surely my fans wouldn't want Rhea's demise to be any other way.

## 26

## CHAPTER 26

Springtime at Mom's house reminded me of my childhood. The garden flowers bloomed full and bright. The grapefruits were abundant and slowly developing their deep red color of their deliciously juicy flesh. And best of all, the butterflies they attracted always welcomed me home.

Even my old bedroom felt like the best times of my upbringing. The times where mom and dad were happy together, and loneliness hadn't yet overtaken me. Even as blissful childhood memories flooded me, I refused to stay in that room by myself for too long.

I no longer found comfort in being by myself or locking myself up behind a closed door in utter isolation. Nolan had often used the excuse of protecting me to justify keeping me away from other or getting too close to people, and I had willingly obliged, believing he knew best.

Not anymore.

The old, worn four-seater sofa in the family room called to me and that's what I had made my sanctuary for the last few weeks. I wanted to be in there when Mom walked past to tend to her garden. I wanted to be outside with her in the fresh air and enjoy the warm sunshine. Being present while she cooked my favorite traditional East Asia dishes meant more to me than it did to her. I missed her cooking and took delight in the aroma of the spices and herbs absorbing into the fabric of my clothes, instead of the latest designer fragrance.

Now when I look in the mirror, I'm not adjusting my false lashes or reapplying lip stain. I'm admiring my strength to get up and look at myself, unaltered by a splash of water to the glass.

Instead of fawning over a glass trophy with my name etched into it, I admire the scar it left on my temple and the uneven eyelid that resulted from it. As those flaws marked the strength, I had to survive something I never thought I would.

I would look back at the professional photos I've taken and the symmetrical features that got me to where I was professionally, but admire the brave, capable, determined woman within that assured I would make it to where I am today.

She was the true beauty, the genuine hero of the story. She deserved so much more credit than I had ever given her. And from now on, I vowed to never question her decisions because she proved her intentions were to keep me safe and sane.

If anyone truly deserved an award, it would be her. And not for her beauty, influence, or identity, but purely for her heroism.

There had been many nights where I met my reflection and confronted the physical trauma that took the form of various versions of me. Like a stack of dominos, each beautiful yet battered spectral figure stood one before the other, mimicking me as I stared wide-eyed at the countless wound alterations.

Nothing, not even the image of a sickly pale Nolan and the leaking black goop that oozed from his eyes, would keep me from my reflection. There were times I imagined his torn forearms reaching through the glass to grasp me, but the fear quickly left my system when I realized he no longer held power over me, and any of his appearances might as well be nothing other than a figment of my fractured imagination. Even if they weren't my mind playing tricks on me, seeing him struggle to get my attention empowered me to smile even brighter.

Like being pushed into the lockers by the bully in high school, I may rehash that painful experience now and then, but ultimately, I smile at how far I've come and how much I learned. And no matter how much I tried to analyze the psychology behind any of our actions, I was no Carl Jung, and settled on one fact—

The experience had pried my eyes wide open.

While sitting on the sofa, laptop on my lap, Mom entered from the hall. She tucked a few of her grey hairs into the fiery red messy bun on the back of her head. "Gonna pick some herbs for dinner. Wanna join?"

Before I could answer, she came around the back of the sofa and wrapped me in a comforting hug. No matter how many times she enveloped me in her arms, I savored each one. Wanting to feel her nurturing warmth was part of what drove me to get up off those cold, white tiles and get back home.

Only after she broke the embrace did I answer, "I'll be right behind you." I kept the smile as she exited the sliding glass door and disappeared into the backyard amongst the kaleidoscope of black and yellow butterflies.

I searched through the dozens of unread emails, ignoring most of the headlines about Joselyn Murphy being arrested after trying to flee to California. I trashed all the mail offering compensation for an exclusive interview about my ordeal and noted all the fan mail instead. But out of dozens of emails, the one that stood out amongst them came from SSL. The subject line read: New Opportunity with Salty Saddle Leggings.

Out of curiosity, I opened the email. It didn't surprise me to see they were offering a new contract to continue as their spokesperson, but this time for their new athletic leggings they were calling, "Survivor runners." The tone of the email was nothing short of opportunistic.

I added it to the growing trash folder and opened an email from a longtime fan to prevent my blood from boiling.

The message contained a color pencil drawing of me surrounded by flowers imbedded in the body email. The look on my face was content, the red hair draped my shoulders like a warm blanket, and the smile on my face was infectious.

The only text was a caption stating, "Peachy."

**27**

— ◆ —

## EPILOGUE

Since returning home to mom, I had first avoided sleep and then grew to dread it. Sleeping seemed to be the closest I've ever come to visiting that ethereal realm again, and as real as that place was, when I had been forced to wander it, the presence of it in my dreams only reminded me how close to death I had come.

The darkness of that place was not as welcoming as I assumed after hearing accounts from people online who claimed to experience near death experiences and the like. The dark, misty space was the opposite of extended meadows, golden sunshine, and brilliant rainbows they used to describe the afterlife.

Even as spacious as the mysterious realm was, in my dreams or otherwise, the fog crept along my body forcing me to fight the claustrophobic feeling, nonetheless. And I was no stranger to claustrophobia and it's crushing claws and suffocating presence.

But tight spaces aside, it wasn't the pitch blackness or the unnerving silence of the realm that prevented me from wanted to return, it was the fear of seeing him. Nolan didn't have a chance to escape that hell, unlike me he had no body to come back to. He would be forever trapped there. Who's to say he wouldn't use his time to wait for another chance to trap what remained of my soul.

Who knew how long he'd try to anchor me down and pull me back into his embrace.

Yet, in my nightmares, time seemed to slip me back into the place I wished not to go. And every time I'm there, confusion and fear overtake me and all I do is run. Run and search for a pinprick of light to steer me back to the physical state and back to the safety of mom's house.

Only when I'm dreaming do I convince myself that a shadow of me had been trapped in the astral plane. And the Rhea who was trapped ran and searched for the sliver of what was left of my soul I had abandoned there.

The thought sent a chill through me, even though it was only a fear.

I had yet to encounter Nolan in my nightmares, but the anticipation of him appearing at any moment to ambush me and pin me down was enough to put my senses on high alert. That anxiety, stress, and the unknown was already nightmarish.

Upon awakening, I would always question myself and my sanity. I shake the unease only after reminding myself I had just woken up from a dream even though that place is more real than real.

He's still there. I know because I have seen him when he joins me in my reflection. Haunting me just like the other Rhea had. But he's not reaching out to me for help or assistance, his aim is to pull me back in his embrace, and he would never give up. In life, he was the kind of guy who always went after what he wanted and very seldomly failed at acquiring it. Would he be the same in death?

Still, he was there. Still, he was with me. I would see him over my shoulder whenever I caught a glimpse of myself in a mirror, a window, or even a stagnant puddle of water. He watched me, remaining a short distance behind me, glaring at me through the reflection with such vile in his murky eyes.

At first, I had ignored his presence, hoping that planting myself in reality would make him disappear. But soon I grew to understand that he would be a part of me for a while and shaking him wouldn't be as easy as abandoning him in the ghostly darkness.

His appearance seemed to transform or disintegrate each time I see him. As time went on, he would get more and more ugly and menacing. Any recognizable human quality slowly drained from him and turned him into a shrunken monster.

Overtime, I no longer feared him and his random appearances. I could see that he had no strength to do any harm to me physically and would eventually be seen as nothing more than a nuisance before disappearing all together.

I told myself that I would only see him if I went looking.

In no time, I began to smile at my own reflection, accepting what fate had thrown me. The scars, the permanent nerve damage to my eyelid that made it appear slightly smaller than the other, the knowledge I had acquired through an unusually and vigorous process.

I looked at my experience as another tool of gaining knowledge on something I had purposely turned a blind eye to.

But it was that acceptance that changed things.

Having just celebrated another year of good health and contentment, and the fact that the hand of justice had come down on Joselyn for her part in my predicament and for not allowing me to get help in an emergency, I was floating high. Although one hundred and twenty days in jail and a substantial fine was what she was up against, it was a start in the right direction.

Feeling safe and secure could finally be a thing after months of adjusting to not having Nolan dictating every moment of my life and career. Although it was tough to adapt to the changes, I knew it was possible.

After a lengthy warm shower, I contemplated cutting and dying my hair to look more like my late grandmother than the well-known online personality. With a towel wrapped around my damp body, I swiped my hand across the mirror to clear the condensation. I stared at my sopping long, red locks and imagined how different I would look without them.

But I couldn't contemplate for long, as a shadowy figure behind me in my reflection swooped by. I turned to make sure I had in fact saw what I thought I had. When I pivoted, I half expected to see nothing but the towel bar behind me. However, I stood stunned as the familiar apparition of Nolan and his grotesque body was there hunched over in the room with me.

I stifled my scream, not wanting to worry mom who roamed the area just outside the bathroom and reminded myself that Nolan no longer held any power over me. He was dead and I killed him. His ghost, much like my own, was limited in how much it affected physical space.

Still, my nerves were humming throughout my body putting me on high alert.

I sneered at the shadowy figure. "You shouldn't be here."

The ghost only shook his head, holding onto itself as if the joints of his body were calcified and prevented fluid movement.

His face was unrecognizable except for the sharp jawline and hairline, which were the only ways I could identify him otherwise.

His deep, hallow eye sockets stared through my soul even though I couldn't distinguish his once piercing steel blues.

An uneasiness crept through me at the fact that I was staring at the shadowy manifestation of the man who tried to overtake and ruin my life. And the most anxiety came when it hit me that he was staring at me as well, communicating even if nonverbally.

What did this mean? Was he able to make a change to have the ability to be seen beyond my nightmares? Will he continue to haunt me like the ghost he was? Or worse yet, would he always be here, never to return to that dark, misty realm?

I tightened the towel around my body mostly to feel a sense of security that was lacking. I needed to hold something tightly in my fist to prevent my fingers from absentmindedly tapping to relieve the built-up stress.

"What do you want?" I finally asked, watching as the dark mists hovered in the corner of the bathroom. "There's nothing here for you so you might as well fuck off!"

"Rhea?" Mom's stern voice called from the other side of the closed and locked door. "Is everything okay?"

I turned to the door, quickly contemplating if I should confide in her or not. I chose against it, not ready to admit that I might not be able to shake Nolan's ghostly presence. "I'm fine. I'll be out in a moment."

She didn't respond, but I knew her suspicions had not left. If I guessed correctly, she was probably still near the door with her ear to it, listening and trying to figure out who I was talking to. She was a smart woman. I'm sure she noticed that I had left my phone on the sofa in the family room and had no way of speaking to anyone in the bathroom but myself.

I didn't want to worry her, and I didn't want to make a big deal out of whatever I was going through, as it was still under my control. There was nothing to worry about ... yet.

When my eyes went back to the corner of the brightly lit bathroom, the misty shadow was no longer there. A part of me was relieved to no longer have to confront that dark past, but the other part questioned what this could mean for me and my future.

I quickly dressed and wrapped my damp hair in a towel before exiting the bathroom only to meet Mom's crossed arms and concerned stare.

"What's going on, Rhea?" She didn't even blink her brown eyes while she waited for my answer.

"I'm fine, Mom." I forced a grin and maneuvered passed her to get to the family room and pretend that my statement was true. "You don't have to worry."

"Who were you talking to?" She followed. Her arms remained cross around her petite body as her attitude made her five-foot-eight stature towered over me like a colossal giant.

"Just talking to myself, it's nothing." I dismissed her worry by swiping the air with my hand and took a seat on the sofa near my phone.

She gave me the side-eye, indicating she wasn't a fool. "How often do you tell yourself to fuck off, hmm?"

"Mom!"

"I'm only repeating what I heard you say." Her eyes softened and she dropped her arms to her sides. "Tell me what's going on."

"I keep having nightmares about Nolan," I admitted, refusing to look into her eyes in case she had the urge to throw me a judging glare.

"Aw, Rhea honey." She groaned and sat beside me on the sofa. "It's normal for someone who's been through what you've been through to feel some lingering unpleasant feelings. This is why I encourage you to stick with counseling. Continue to talk to your counselor about these things and keep up with Dr. Desiree and your health. It will help." She squeezed my knee to comfort me. "But what does your nightmares have to do with you yelling in the bathroom?"

I avoided looking at her but shook my head, sighing as I confessed, "I think I saw Nolan in the bathroom with me or at least his ghost."

"Ok." She nodded, taking a pause as she normally does when discussing heavy topics to carefully think of her next words. "What was he doing or saying?"

"He didn't say anything, but he was watching me. Almost like he refused to give up. Like no matter what, he had a mission to accomplish, and that mission is to reclaim my soul." I knew it sounded weird as soon as it left my lips, but she wanted to know, and I was set on being honest.

"I know it might sound crazy, but I believed you when you told me you watched a repeat of your life with him from your ghost's perspective." She paused and gently squeezed my knee again. "I had an out of body experience recently too that led me to leave your father. It took me opening my eyes and seeing what was right in front of me to act and change my life for the better."

"What? I never knew that." I finally mustered the courage to look at her and saw the glistening tears hovering on her eyelids.

"It's true." She frowned. "We hid a lot of things from you for your safety. We love you and didn't want you to see how bad things had become. But I also think it's important for you to understand that just because things look okay on the outside doesn't mean that's truly the case. Sometimes we hide the truth for various reasons, but it's okay to admit when things are wrong."

"I would've never guessed." I shook my head, realizing that her and I were alike on so many levels. I never would have known this if I continued to keep my distance. I always believed she was out of touch and wouldn't understand. I always thought it was good to keep my distance from my parents because they disapproved of my relationship and career choices, but maybe I had been missing out.

"Sometimes it takes going through something difficult to see the truth of the matter." She wrapped and arm around me and gave me a soothing embrace. "I'm proud of you, Rhea. I knew you would open your eyes soon enough."

"Thank you."

"And as for Nolan," she continued. "Sometimes the ghosts of those who hurt us most will linger around to haunt us. It would be hard to shake for a while, and some days will be worse than others, but I have faith that you will come out victorious on the other side. You never let him get the best of you, and you won't start now. Trust me, that ghost will fade away eventually."

She left me with a smile and boost of power I needed. Mom's conversations were better than any professional at the moment. But she was right, I knew this too would pass and become nothing more than a fleeting memory in due time.

As I stood to follow her into the kitchen and help prepare dinner, something on the sofa caught my eye and startled me. I turned to get a better look and held back my gasp. Sitting in the spot where Mom had been sitting was the fragile, see-through, full-bodied image of Joselyn. She sat crossed legged in her prim and proper high fashion attire, high heels, and all, glaring at me with her vacant, sunken eyes.

www.ingramcontent.com/pod-product-compliance
Lightning Source LLC
Chambersburg PA
CBHW070957190726
48292CB00004B/1488